Heartland

Holding Fast

Heartland

Share every moment. . . .

Heartland

❧

Holding Fast

by **Lauren Brooke**

GRANT MacEWAN SCHOOL

SCHOLASTIC INC.

New York   Toronto   London   Auckland   Sydney
Mexico City   New Delhi   Hong Kong   Buenos Aires

With special thanks to Gill Harvey

If you purchased this book without a cover, you should be aware that this book is stolen property. It was reported as "unsold and destroyed" to the publisher, and neither the author nor the publisher has received any payment for this "stripped book."

No part of this publication may be reproduced in whole or in part, or stored in a retrieval system, or transmitted in any form or by any means, electronic, mechanical, photocopying, recording, or otherwise, without written permission of the publisher. For information regarding permission, write to Scholastic Inc., Attention: Permissions Department, 557 Broadway, New York, NY 10012.

ISBN 0-439-42511-5

Heartland series created by Working Partners Ltd, London.

Copyright © 2004 by Working Partners Ltd.
Published by Scholastic Inc. All rights reserved.

SCHOLASTIC and associated logos are trademarks and/or registered trademarks of Scholastic Inc. HEARTLAND is a trademark and/or registered trademark of Working Partners Ltd.

12 11 10 9 8 7 6 5 4 3 2   4 5 6 7 8 9/0
Printed in the U.S.A.   40
First printing, June 2004

*To Sheila Gill, who has taught
Amy everything she knows about
Bach Flower Remedies.*

Chapter One

"I can see them! Over there!" Amy said excitedly, pointing to the far end of the row of expectant faces at the airport baggage claim.

"Where?" asked Amy's sister Lou, craning her neck.

Amy pointed again to where the two familiar figures stood. Lou beckoned to her boyfriend, Scott, while Amy grinned and waved, then pushed her luggage cart a little faster.

"Ty! Grandpa!" Amy reached Ty and let go of the cart to fling her arms around him. He laughed into her hair and held her tight.

"Oh, it's so good to see you!" Amy exclaimed, letting go of Ty to give Jack a big hug, too. "I've really missed you both!"

"Not as much as we've missed *you*," said Ty. "We're relieved that Australia let us have you back."

"Of course it did," said Amy, as Lou and Scott came up to join in the round of welcoming hugs. "You didn't think I'd want to stay with Dad, did you?"

Ty looked down at her, a smile lighting up his soft green eyes. "It crossed my mind. But only for — oh, about two and a half seconds."

Amy laughed and reached for his hand. There had never been any doubt in her own mind, not even for an instant. This was where she wanted to be — back in Virginia with Ty and Grandpa, heading home to Heartland and the horses she worked with. It had been wonderful to see her father Tim's beautiful stables, to meet his wife, Helena, and their young daughter, Lily, but it had made Amy realize that Heartland was where she belonged.

"The car's in short-term parking," said Jack, picking up Amy's bag. "Let's get going. You must be exhausted."

Lou nodded. "You could say that," she agreed. "It was such a long flight. Seventeen hours, and even with Scott's shoulder for a pillow, I couldn't sleep."

They all crowded into Jack Bartlett's station wagon with their luggage and set off. Amy was squashed in next to Ty in the front seat, and she wrapped his arm around her shoulder so they better fit in the cramped space. She was tired and jet-lagged from the long journey, but her happiness at seeing him had given her a burst of energy.

"Now seems like the perfect time to give me an update on everything that's been happening," she said. "You haven't been overdoing it, have you?" She gave him a knowing glance.

"I'm fine," Ty assured her. "I've just been doing as much as I can, and no more. My endurance is slowly coming back. I'm feeling better. Honest, I am."

Amy looked at Ty's face and believed him. It seemed incredible that only a few months ago he had been lying in the hospital. He'd been in critical condition after being trapped in a horse barn following a vicious tornado that had caused the roof to collapse. Amy had wondered if he would ever wake up, if he would ever be a part of their work at Heartland again. But here he was, looking tan from his outdoor life, despite the winter chill. Amy thought how great it was to be home and for things to be back to normal.

"How's Dazzle?" she asked.

Dazzle was a mustang stallion who had arrived at Heartland while Ty was still in a coma. Dazzle had been taken straight from the wild freedom of the western plains, and it hadn't been easy for Amy to connect with him. But Ty had developed a special bond with Dazzle when he first returned from the hospital. They both had a lot of adjusting to do, and Ty and the horse seemed to gain strength from each other.

Ty smiled. "He's doing great," he said. "It won't be long before he's ready to go back to his owners."

That was the way things worked at Heartland — horses came to be gentled or to be treated for problems, but they would always leave again to make room for others. Amy knew it would be tough for Ty to see Dazzle go. They had been through a lot together.

She squeezed his hand. "I'm glad I'm back," she whispered.

❧

As they turned onto the gravel drive that led to Heartland, Amy felt as though she'd been away for months rather than a couple of weeks. Despite her exhaustion, she couldn't wait to see all the horses. She told herself she'd take a quick walk through the stables and then head straight to bed. But when they pulled up to the whitewashed farmhouse, she could tell that there was no chance of that — not for quite some time.

A crowd of people stood outside the farmhouse, waving and cheering as the station wagon came to a halt. There was Ben, Heartland's other stable hand, and Amy's best friend Soraya with her boyfriend, Matt, who was Scott's brother. Ty's mom was standing there, too, next to Grandpa's friend, Nancy. Amy stared at everyone in disbelief. She wasn't sure why there was such a welcoming party — they hadn't been away *that* long!

Amy and Lou jumped out and everyone quickly gathered around. After a big round of hugs and kisses, Nancy clapped her hands to get everyone's attention. She was wearing an apron over her blue jeans and buttoned shirt, and Amy guessed she'd been cooking. Her heart sank at the idea of a big sit-down meal. She felt too tired to eat. She just wanted to visit the horses before taking a shower and a nap. She glanced sideways at Lou to see her reaction, but her sister was talking excitedly to Scott and his brother.

"Supper's ready," Nancy announced. "You must be starving after that long flight. Come on in."

Amy looked longingly at the stables. After being stuck on a crowded plane for almost twenty hours, she craved the peace of the yard. But Ty put his arm around her, and Amy let him steer her inside to a seat at the kitchen table.

Nancy had been busy. A huge roast chicken sat waiting to be carved, surrounded by crispy roast potatoes. A steaming gravy boat sat next to it, and a big platter of fresh green beans and peas. Nancy looked flushed and happy, her blue eyes sparkling as she handed the carving knife to Grandpa and started dishing out the vegetables.

Amy felt a wave of fatigue wash over her. The smiling faces around the table seemed as though they were far away, chatting in distant voices. A plate of food was placed in front of her, so she picked up her knife and fork and mechanically began to chew a piece of chicken. She could tell it was beautifully cooked, but she had to make a huge effort to keep eating while everyone laughed at Lou's description of their sister Lily.

"Oooh — that was her name for me," she said. "She couldn't say the *L*. And she called Amy *Amee*. She's a real cutie, isn't she, Amy?"

"Sorry?" questioned Amy, coming out of her reverie. "Oh — Lily. Yes, she's sweet."

She gave Lou a small smile. The truth was that it had taken her a while to get used to her half sister. For one thing, she was more accustomed to dealing with horses than toddlers; and finding her place in her father's new family hadn't been easy, either. She listened as Lou talked about Helena and Tim and her trip with Scott across the outback.

As Lou described the amazing red desert landscape, Amy saw her exchange glances with Scott and suspected what was next to come. "We've got something to announce," said Lou, smiling across the table at Heartland's longtime vet. "Scott planned a morning hike to view Ayers Rock. As we watched the sun rise, he proposed. And I said yes. We're engaged!"

Jack got to his feet and reached out to shake Scott's hand. "Well, that's wonderful news," he said, raising his glass. "I have to admit that we had an inkling — that's why Nancy suggested the welcome home party — and it's great to hear we were right. It'll be nice to have you as an official part of the family, Scott. I think we should have a toast. To Lou and Scott!"

"To Lou and Scott!" chorused everyone with a lively chink of glasses.

"I spotted Scott at a jewelry store a few weeks ago," Nancy confessed when the hubbub had died down. "It was right before you'd decided to go on the trip, so when I heard about Australia, I guessed he might propose while you were away. That's why I took a chance and got everyone together. It's so exciting! Now, when's the big day? Have you decided yet?"

Lou looked slightly taken aback. "Oh, we haven't figured out any of the details yet," she said. "It's a bit early for that."

Matt thumped his brother on the shoulder. "Nice work, Scott," he said. "Mom will go crazy over this. You'll have to watch out for her. She'll have a field day organizing everything."

"Actually," Nancy broke in, "it is traditionally the bride's side of the family that does the organizing. Your mother won't have anything to worry about."

"I'm sure she'll pitch in anyway." Matt grinned. "She won't let a little detail like not having any daughters stop her!"

"Well, it can make things quite difficult when both families get involved," Nancy said cautiously. "But I'm sure it will all work out beautifully, if you allow enough time for planning. That's why it's good to set a date nice and early. Isn't that right, Jack?"

Grandpa nodded, a smile stretching clear across his face. Amy thought he looked happier than she'd ever seen him, sitting with Nancy on one side and Lou on the other. "The sooner, the better. Why not?" he said.

But as the conversation bounced around the table with everyone adding some advice, Lou began to look a little uneasy. "Really, we're not making any definite plans yet," she insisted. "I have far too much to deal with at Heartland first. I mean, I just got back."

Amy stared at her sister, the words slowly sinking in. When Lou had told her in Australia that she and Scott were engaged, she hadn't really thought what it could mean. For some reason, she had assumed that Lou being married wouldn't make much difference in their everyday lives. But now it dawned on her for the first time that Lou might be leaving Heartland.

The main course was over at last, and Amy felt relieved as Nancy took her plate away. She thought now might be her chance to slip out and see the horses.

"I'm going to get some air," she said to Ty in a low voice.

Amy got up and headed for the door. She thought how good it would be to see Sundance, Sugarfoot, the little Shetland, Jasmine — all the Heartland residents as well as the new arrivals. She was taking long strides across the yard in the quiet night air when a voice stopped her.

"Amy! Are you OK?" It was Lou.

Amy turned around and smiled wanly. "I'm fine. Just tired. I want to see the horses."

Lou nodded. "I know." She took a deep breath. "It's all a bit much, isn't it? I was looking forward to a lazy evening. I didn't expect there to be such a fuss about our engagement." She paused and took a step closer to Amy. "Are you sure you're OK with all of this?"

"Of course I'm sure. Why wouldn't I be?" Amy asked carefully.

"Well — because a lot of things are going to change."

Amy was silent. She couldn't lie to Lou; her sister knew her too well for that. Amy really wanted to launch into a list of questions: How would things change? And how much? But at the same time, she didn't want to spoil Lou's excitement. "It won't be really soon, though, will it?" she asked eventually.

"No," said Lou. "We don't want to set a date yet, despite what everyone's saying. All this talk about the wedding — it's like Scott and I are suddenly the guests of honor in our own family or something. It's too much, too soon. And, really, I'm so jet-lagged that all I want to do is sleep."

"I know what you mean," said Amy, feeling fatigue seeping through her.

Lou sighed. "I'd better go back in. Nancy's serving dessert." She looked at Amy, a pleading expression in her eyes. "You won't be long, will you?"

Amy looked down toward the barns, then smiled back at Lou. She knew she couldn't leave Lou to deal with all that attention on her own. She took Lou's arm. "The horses can wait," she said, and they went back inside.

Amy sat back down next to Ty. He threw her a questioning glance and she just shook her head with a smile. Nancy was cutting into an enormous homemade blueberry cheesecake. Amy was so tired she was afraid she might fall asleep at the table. She pictured her face diving straight into her plate. Still, she couldn't resist dessert. She gave the older woman a warm smile. Nancy sure could cook.

The party atmosphere calmed down a little as everyone ooohed and aahed over the cheesecake. Soraya and Matt told everyone about the day they went fishing with Soraya's aunt and uncle at a lake in the mountains while Amy had been away. Amy couldn't picture Soraya handling the bait, but it still sounded like fun. They were obviously getting along really well as a couple. Amy thought about being back at school on Monday, and she wondered if Matt and Soraya would want her hanging around with them now that they were so close.

"We can go down to see Dazzle after dinner if you're not too tired," Ty offered, breaking in on her thoughts.

"That would be great," Amy responded, smiling at him. "I need to see Sundance, too, and maybe the new boarders."

"Of course," Ty said, scraping the last bite of cheesecake from his plate.

Finally, the meal was over. Amy offered to help clear the table.

Nancy wouldn't hear of it. "You need to unwind and rest," she said briskly, wiping her hands on her apron. "Go on, off you go. I can manage."

Feeling relieved, Amy slipped out and made her way down to the stable yard. She quickly found Ty, who was getting a flashlight from the tack room.

"Dazzle's still in the bottom paddock," he explained, and they set off down the main path, and past the newly repaired barn. Seeing the barn and the winter shadows, Amy could hardly make out the addition of the new beams that now shouldered the weight of the roof. She thought it was almost as though the nightmare had never happened — but only *almost*. The memories of that terrifying night would never completely be erased.

As they walked to the paddocks, Amy was aware of Ty limping a little beside her — so much better than he had been, but still not completely healed.

"So, how's your physical therapy going?" she asked, her voice sounding brighter than her thoughts.

"It's hard," Ty admitted. "But the more I work at it, the quicker I improve. The doctors all say I'm ahead of schedule. I'll be as good as new before long. Promise."

Ty trained the flashlight over the fence as they approached the paddock. A handsome blue roan stallion emerged out of the shadows toward them, his nostrils blowing clouds of steam in the cold air.

"Hey, boy," Ty called softly. "Come and say hi to Amy."

Dazzle snorted in welcome and thrust his head over the fence. Ty fished in his pocket for some alfalfa cubes and held them in the palm of his hand. Dazzle stretched out his neck and delicately lipped up the cubes one by one, gently blowing over Ty's hand. Amy's heart warmed as she reached out to scratch his neck. This Dazzle was so different from the wild, desperate creature that had arrived at Heartland almost straight from the deserts of Nevada, furious to have been deprived of his freedom. Amy still couldn't help feeling that the desert was where he truly belonged, but that was no longer a possibility for him. What was important now was that he had learned to respect and enjoy human company.

Dazzle nudged Ty, hoping for more treats, and Ty laughed. "He knows I'm a pushover," he said.

He fed the stallion another handful, then he and Amy walked back up to the stable block. They did a round of the barn, saying hello to all the horses before finishing up in the front yard.

"Come and meet Molly," said Ty. "She's only been here a couple of days. I've been letting her settle in."

He stopped at the first stall and Amy peered past him. A sleek-limbed bright bay mare was dozing at the back of the stall, resting one hind leg. She woke as Ty switched the light on, and she turned her head to give a deep nicker of welcome. Amy took in her slightly dished face and big, gentle eyes. She was a beauty.

"She's lovely," said Amy. "And she seems so friendly. What's her history?"

"She's part quarter horse, part Arab," said Ty. "Her owner's name is Eloise Beatson. She's about Lou's age, and she says she mostly uses Molly for trail riding."

"So what's the problem?" asked Amy. "She looks like she'd be a great ride."

"Yeah," agreed Ty. "But she's been difficult recently. Eloise says she was riding her through a creek a month or so ago and she stepped on a sharp stone that sliced right into Molly's frog. The cut developed into an abscess, which Eloise treated with antibiotics. But when Eloise started riding her again, Molly wasn't the same.

She'll spook at anything now, even things like waving long grass or shadows. It seems like she's completely lost her confidence."

"Poor girl," murmured Amy.

She let herself into the stall and ran her hand lightly over the bay's shoulder. Molly looked around, flicking one of her ears back. Amy studied her. The lines of her body were relaxed, and trust shone out of her large dark eyes. There were no signs at all of bad temper or a difficult nature.

"She doesn't look like the type to bear a grudge," she commented.

"That's what I thought," Ty agreed. "She's sensitive, but there's nothing mean about her."

Amy worked her fingers in little circles up Molly's neck and felt the mare relax almost immediately. She was clearly a horse that enjoyed connecting with humans and responded well to attention. "What was it like when Eloise left her?"

"She was pretty upset. She called after her for about half an hour," said Ty. "We gave her some Rescue Remedy, and Ben stayed close by, doing stable work and checking on her. She calmed down after a while, but she's loyal. There's no doubting the bond between her and Eloise."

Amy smiled. She'd missed this so much in recent

months — being with Ty and discussing the horses with him, knowing that they understood each other. First there had been Ty's coma, then her trip to Australia. But now they were both back, and life could return to normal at last.

Chapter Two

The chestnut gelding and his rider seemed to fly around the training ring. The jumps were more than a yard high, but the horse's ears were pricked forward and, with his rider's help, he judged each one perfectly.

Amy applauded as the pair cleared the final fence and slowed to a controlled canter, then a trot.

"Bravo!" she called. "You and Red look fantastic. It's so good to see him in full form!"

Ben rode over, patting Red on the neck as he did so.

"Thanks, Amy," he said. "Things *are* going well. I think we stand a really good chance at Brideswell next Saturday."

It was Tuesday evening, and Amy had been back at school for two days. It was a shock to the system after her vacation, but at least she'd managed to keep up with

all her assignments while she was away. Even so, she'd
been especially glad to escape school that afternoon —
her French class had seemed to drag on forever.

She smiled up at Ben. "Well, I hope you bring home
the blue ribbon," she said.

"We will if Red keeps this up," said Ben. "Actually, I
was hoping to take a couple of days off next week before
the show. I was thinking of trailering him over early, so
he has time to adjust to the show grounds."

Amy bit her lip. She wasn't sure they could spare Ben
so easily while she was at school, especially since Ty still
had several physical therapy appointments during the
week. Still, she knew he fully deserved a break after all
the work he'd put in. "I'll need to check with Ty," she
said. "Just to make sure he'll be able to cover —"

To her surprise, Ben interrupted her. "Oh, never
mind," he said. "I should have known Heartland would
have to come first."

Abruptly, he turned Red and rode off down the training ring at a brisk trot.

Amy's mouth dropped open. She watched Ben ride
away and wondered whether to call him back; but he
was already working at winding down with Red, taking
him over some smaller jumps to finish the session. Amy
turned and went back to the barn, feeling slightly hurt
and bewildered.

It wasn't like Ben to be so abrupt. She knew he had

had his own share of difficult times recently. Red had contracted the flu and hadn't been able to compete for weeks, and with Ty in the hospital, Ben had worked really hard around the yard, even taking on some of Amy's chores so that she could concentrate on treating the horses. Then he'd missed his chance with Soraya, who had started going out with Matt. To top things off, Amy had gone to Australia, leaving Ben with an even heavier workload. No wonder he was aggravated. Amy knew she should talk to Ty and figure out a way for Ben to get some days off before the show.

As she walked up the path, Amy heard Lou calling her from the farmhouse door. Her sister motioned to her to come in.

"What is it?" Amy asked as soon as she opened the door.

"There's been a call," said Lou as Amy followed her into the kitchen. "It's kind of . . . interesting. I wanted to talk it through with you before we say anything to anyone else."

Amy was intrigued. "Really? What kind of call?"

Lou picked up a news article from a Web page that was lying on the table. "Do you remember this?" she asked, handing the paper to Amy.

Amy looked at the date at the top of the page, and her heart began to pound. It was the day after the tornado — the day when it seemed that her whole world was falling apart. She read the headline: HERO POLICE OFFICER MAKES DRAMATIC RESCUE. She glanced at Lou and shook her head. With all that had happened, the last thing she'd wanted to do right after the storm was follow the news. Even during the hours she spent in the hospital, she hadn't been able to focus on anything but Ty.

"Read on," said Lou.

Amy scanned the article. "'Sergeant Mark García made a heroic rescue of three local children who had been trapped in an overturned car in a demolition lot last night. The boys, all aged 12, were sitting in a scrapped car when the storm struck. The car was flipped over by one of the series of tornadoes that accompanied the thunderstorm. The impact crushed the car roof, jamming the doors shut. One boy's leg was broken in three places, but thanks to Sergeant García's swift work, no further injuries occurred. All three boys are now in good condition in Riverside Hospital. Two are expected to return home this evening.

"'Sergeant García's valiant rescue work did come at a price. His trusted patrol horse was injured in the recovery of the boys . . .'"

Amy put the paper down. "What happened to his horse? Is that what the call was about?"

Lou nodded. "Apparently Venture — that's the horse's name — seemed to have healed from his injuries, but he just hasn't been the same. The vets are puzzled, because all the tests suggest he should be healthy. But he still acts like he's in pain, and he hates being ridden, even by Sergeant García. I think the police are turning to us as a last resort. If we can't do anything with him, they'll just retire him. That's really all I know."

Amy thought for a moment. Any reminder of that night would be difficult for everyone at Heartland, but especially for Ty. "I'm not sure if Ty would be up to it," she said slowly. "It's hard enough knowing the history of some of the horses, but this might hit too close to home. I'd like to help Venture, but it should be Ty's decision."

"I think that's a good idea," agreed Lou. "I can foresee a few other problems, too. The papers are still following the story, so there'd be the potential of a lot of media attention. While that's not all bad, we should consider the fact that Venture will have already received the best treatment money can buy. Police horses are valuable, and they go through a long training process, so the force will do their best to keep their horses working. We might not be able to do anything for him, which could look bad. You know how the papers twist everything."

Amy frowned. "I'm not so worried about that side of things," she said. She realized that her instinct to help a horse in pain was kicking in already, despite the obstacles. "It's Venture that counts, not what the papers say. We *might* be able to help."

Lou smiled. "I thought you might say that," she said.

"I'd need to check him out, though," said Amy. "I mean, there isn't much to go on. If Ty's OK with it, I'd like to see Venture — and maybe his partner."

"That's a good idea," said Lou. "Let me know what Ty says. I told them I'd call back tomorrow." She looked around as Jack came through the door with Nancy. "Hi," she greeted them.

"Hello, Lou," said Nancy, kissing her on the cheek. "And you, Amy."

Amy smiled and lifted her face for Nancy to kiss as well. Jack took off his coat and then helped Nancy with hers.

"Oh, thank you, Jack," she said, shrugging out of the sleeves and handing it to him. Nancy then pulled a big plastic sealed container out of her bag. "I know how busy you all are," she said. "So I cooked some pasta for us all to have for supper. It just needs heating up."

Lou looked taken aback. "Oh," she said. "You didn't need to do that, Nancy. I made a quiche this afternoon. It just needs to be heated up, too."

There was an edge to Lou's voice, and Amy looked at her sister in surprise.

"Oh, I am sorry, Lou," said Nancy. "I just assumed . . ."

Lou did not respond. She simply raised her eyebrows dramatically. Nancy flushed and glanced quickly at Grandpa.

"Two dinners! We are doing well," said Jack Bartlett with a chuckle. "Perhaps we could have the quiche tomorrow, Lou. That'll save you some time, won't it? And there's room in the fridge."

Lou pursed her lips, then forced them into a smile. "I guess so," she said, and took the container from Nancy. "Thanks, Nancy." She tipped the creamy pasta dish into a saucepan and put it on low heat on the stove. "Could you keep an eye on that for me, Amy?" she asked. "I'm just going upstairs to change."

Lou left the kitchen. Amy watched her go, feeling baffled. It wasn't like Lou to take offense over such a little thing — and besides, it was obvious that Nancy was only trying to help. Amy stirred the pasta with a wooden spoon, sniffing it appreciatively. It smelled delicious.

After a while, Lou came back downstairs and helped Amy serve dinner. She was quieter than usual, but otherwise she seemed fine. Amy decided it was probably best not to ask about it. Lou was as busy as the rest of them, settling back into the Heartland routine after their trip. It was hardly surprising that she was tense.

The next morning, Amy got up early to work with the horses before school, as usual. It hadn't taken her long to get back into the cadence of her stable work — almost as though she'd never been away. She dressed quickly and went down to the front yard. Molly had her head over her stall door and whinnied a welcome when she saw Amy.

Amy smiled. Molly seemed to be such an affectionate horse.

"Hi there, girl," she greeted the mare. "You're up bright and early!"

She unbolted the stall door and gently clipped a halter on the horse's head. Over the last couple of days, she had been getting to know the mare by spending time in her stall, grooming her, and giving her a targeted massage technique called T-touch. This had reaffirmed her first impressions. Molly was responsive and friendly and seemed to take pleasure in people's company. Although she hadn't ridden her yet, Amy suspected that Molly's problem lay in some kind of breakdown in the relationship with her owner, and to get to the root of it she needed to establish a strong bond of trust with the mare herself.

Amy led her down to the smaller training ring and unclipped her halter. Molly remained close to her, nosing her jacket. *OK, girl, we need to get down to business*, Amy thought to herself. She drew herself up tall, assuming an aggressive stance, and motioned for Molly to go away. Molly threw up her head and ambled across the ring, but she soon stopped and looked back at Amy. *Do you really want me to go away?* she seemed to question.

Amy smiled. Join up involved driving a horse away until she chose human company of her own free will — but with Molly, there wasn't much doubt about what she wanted. She was quite happy to stay with Amy from the outset. Amy flapped her arms and ran at her anyway, knowing that a successful join up would still be useful.

Molly snorted and trotted off around the ring. Amy drove her into a canter and kept her going for a few minutes. It didn't take long for Molly to show the classic signs that she wanted to be with Amy — first flicking her ear, then lowering her head and making chewing motions. The next stage followed with the same ease. The mare reacted to Amy's turned figure and sought her company in the center of the ring. Amy turned and patted the mare's neck, then clipped the lead rope to her halter again.

"Good girl," she murmured as Molly followed her to the gate. "That's a good start, isn't it?"

She took the mare back to the front yard, deciding what to do next. There was little problem joining up with Molly and working with her from the ground, but riding her would be the real test. Amy wanted to make sure that the mare trusted her completely before she did so. The last thing she wanted was to set their progress back by taking things too quickly.

✎

As Amy let Molly back into her stall, she spotted Ben marching up from the barn, carrying empty feed buckets. He was striding along with his head down, a preoccupied expression on his face.

"Morning, Ben!" Amy called.

Ben raised his head. "Oh, hi."

He went to the yard tap and turned it on, placing one of the buckets under it. Amy remembered that she wanted to check with Ty about his schedule. She noticed that Ben still seemed tense.

"How's it going?" she asked, keeping her voice light. "I've finished with Molly. I can take over the feeds now, if you like."

Ben straightened up, shaking his head. "Don't worry about it. I've done the front yard. I'm just cleaning these buckets out, then I was going to take care of the back barn and start mucking out those stalls. I'm used to doing everything — it won't take me long." He hesitated, then added gruffly, "Sorry about last night. I was pretty rude."

"That's OK," said Amy. "Forget it."

She went to get a pitchfork and wheelbarrow. Ben's words echoed in her ears: *I'm used to doing everything.* Amy felt a flash of guilt. Ben had seemed so willing to work hard over the last few months. Had they all taken him for granted?

She was in the middle of mucking out Jasmine's stall

when she heard the sound of Mrs. Baldwin's car pulling up the drive.

"Morning," Amy called, as Ty got out of the car and waved good-bye to his mother. He came over and gave Amy a kiss over the half door.

"How far did you get?" he asked. "You'll need to get ready for school soon."

"There are still the last two on this block and the back barn," said Amy. "But I think Ben's already started them. And he's done the feeds." She paused. "Is Ben OK, by the way? Did something happen while I was away?"

Ty raised an eyebrow. "Why? What happened?"

"He just seems a bit on edge," said Amy and told him about their exchange in the training ring the night before. "Then this morning, he was talking about getting the jobs over with, and he sounded really spent. I feel bad. What do you have going next week? Is there any way he could take off Thursday and Friday?"

Ty nodded. "Yeah, sure. I'll confirm it with the hospital, but that sounds fine. If he's stressed, I'm sure a good showing at Brideswell would help."

"That's what I was thinking." Amy nodded in agreement. "Could you sort it out with him while I'm at school?"

"Yeah, I'll do that," said Ty.

Feeling relieved, Amy lifted another forkload of straw, then remembered her conversation with Lou the night before. She checked her watch and decided now was as good a time as any. "There's something else, too," she said.

She chose her words carefully as she told Ty about Venture. She didn't want to sway his decision. "Lou and I were concerned that it might be too difficult for you," she finished, searching Ty's face. "You need to be honest about this."

Ty smiled and touched her arm. "I really appreciate you asking," he said. "But the truth is, I've been lucky. I feel like it's our responsibility to help any horse that was injured in that storm. Heartland's the best place for him."

Amy smiled. "I'm glad," she said. "One of us should see him first, anyway, just to find out what he's like." She set the pitchfork against the barn. "I'd better get going, or I'll be late."

❧

Amy dashed inside for a quick shower and flung on her school clothes before rushing downstairs again. Lou was sitting at the kitchen table with a cup of coffee in front of her, going through the mail.

"Ty says he's up for taking Venture, if the visit goes

OK," Amy told her, grabbing her schoolbag. "Will you let me know if you set something up?"

"Sure," Lou replied. "I'll leave a message on your cell phone."

"OK, thanks," Amy called over her shoulder, and she ran down the driveway to catch the bus.

For once, the morning passed pretty quickly. Amy had geography just before lunch, which she found more interesting than a lot of her other classes. They were learning about environmental issues and how America's wild spaces had shrunk over the years. She thought of Dazzle and realized that millions of creatures all over the world were being forced from their natural habitats. Perhaps Dazzle was lucky after all, she mused — at least the Bureau of Land Management ensured that he had some kind of future, even if it wasn't in the wild. She knew many horses and other species would simply die out.

When the lunchtime bell rang, Amy went outside to check her cell phone. Lou had left a message telling her that she'd pick her up after school for an appointment with Sergeant García, who would show them Venture.

Amy realized she was feeling quite excited about treating the police horse, and she looked for Soraya. Her friend was in the cafeteria, in line for the salad bar.

"Hey, guess what!" said Amy. "Lou and I are going to the police stables tonight!"

"The police stables?" Soraya echoed.

"We might be taking one of their horses," Amy explained. "He was injured in a tornado on the same night as Ty. He never really got better, and they don't know why. He's been in the papers and everything."

Soraya looked at Amy in surprise. "He was injured in the same storm?" she exclaimed. "Geez, Amy, are you going to be OK with that?"

"Why wouldn't I be?" asked Amy. "I've talked to Ty. He doesn't have any problem with it, if that's what you mean."

Soraya smiled. "Sorry. I don't want to interfere or anything," she said gently. "It's just that you've already been through so much because of the storm."

"I know," Amy admitted. "But maybe that's not a bad thing. It might mean that we have something special to offer."

"You're so brave sometimes, Amy," said Soraya, squeezing her friend's arm. "I don't think I could face up to awful memories so easily. I hope it's not too painful for you."

For *her*? Soraya's words sank in, and Amy felt disconcerted as she became aware of her heart beating slightly faster. She'd been worried for Ty, but she hadn't really thought about what she herself would be forced to endure.

She pushed the thought away. This would be different. There was no reason why treating a horse should remind her of visiting Ty when he was motionless in the hospital, of witnessing his first agonizing attempts at rehabilitation. She shook her head and smiled. "I'm not the one who's being brave," she said. "If Ty can handle it, I'm sure I can, too."

Chapter Three

At last the day was over, and Amy went to the parking lot. She spotted Lou's car and climbed in, picking up the map that Lou had placed on the dashboard.

"Where are we going?" she asked, unfolding the map.

"Venture's at a stable on the other side of town," said Lou as they turned onto the highway. "My understanding is that it's where police horses go when they retire, and it's where injuries and other problems are handled, too. Sounds interesting."

It *was* interesting — another place that treated horses, but only police horses. She wondered how different their approach would be.

A tall, broad-shouldered man with short, spiky, dark hair was seated on a bench at the entrance to the stables. Lou lowered her window. "Sergeant García?" When the man nodded, she continued. "I'm Lou Fleming, and this is Amy. We spoke on the phone."

Sergeant García nodded. "Glad you could make it, Ms. Fleming," he said. "You can park just around to the left. I'll follow you."

Lou drove slowly to where he had indicated, giving Amy a chance to look around. The yard was large and immaculately maintained, without a trace of loose straw on the even concrete. She caught a glimpse of a paddock on the right, where four or five horses were grazing peacefully, and a spacious training ring. Whatever techniques they used, Amy realized that Lou was right — as far as Venture's treatment was concerned, no expense would have been spared.

Mark García was standing by the stable block. There was something about his upright posture that made Amy think he was born to be a police officer. Amy appraised him silently. He seemed rather reserved, and it was difficult to see beyond his calm exterior. But he was welcoming enough. His wide-set hazel eyes brightened when he shook their hands, and as they walked around the stable block, he described what had happened on the night of the storm.

"I was on patrol out toward the industrial side of

town. We cover a stretch between two city parks. I'd nearly finished my shift," he explained, "when the storm blew up out of nowhere. I saw a twister and herded people into a park building. Then I went into a garage with Venture. After it passed and everyone was safe, I wanted to get Venture back to the stables. But then I heard screams coming from this junkyard. It was crammed full of scrap metal."

He paused as if trying to recollect events as accurately as possible. "It turned out that the owner's son and some of his friends had gotten caught in the storm. They'd taken shelter in one of the old cars, but a tornado whipped through the yard and turned it over."

Sergeant García talked in a quiet, matter-of-fact way that belied the drama of his words. But for Amy, the description brought back the full horror of the storm. She tried to block out her memories and concentrate on the sergeant's retelling, but she realized she was shaking, her hands clenched.

"The kids were trapped," the policeman continued. "I could see fuel leaking from the car. I called for help, but I knew something had to be done fast. It seemed like the storm was picking up again. So I dismounted and led Venture toward the car."

A frown creased his forehead. "That's when things went wrong. A gust of wind got under a pile of tires, and a couple of them crashed down on Venture's back. He went down on his knees, then scrambled back up right away. It all happened so fast that I wasn't even sure if he'd really been injured."

They stopped outside one of the stalls and Amy read the nameplate: VENTURE. It was a relief to come back to the present.

"Venture! Here, boy," called Sergeant García. He clicked his fingers, and a beautiful dark bay horse of about seventeen hands appeared over the half door. Amy's eyes took in his strong, stocky frame and noble head. She reached up to stroke his neck as the sergeant finished his story.

"His knees had a few cuts and he seemed shaken. I knew I shouldn't ride him until he'd been checked over, so I hooked his reins around my arm while I tried to help the kids. I managed to pry open the car door. Two of the kids scrambled out, and they helped me wrench off the metal that was trapping the third. We got him out, but the poor kid was in a terrible state. It turned out he'd broken his leg in three places. I knew that moving him could make things worse, but it was better than leaving him in that car."

"That must have been a tough decision," remarked Lou.

Mark García gave a small smile. "It's part of the job," he shrugged.

Amy stroked Venture's soft nose. For all his size and strength, the horse had gentle features — a big Roman nose, large, liquid eyes, and a sensitive muzzle, suggesting a patient, willing character.

"What exactly were Venture's injuries?" she asked.

"The knee injuries were superficial, fortunately. His back's been more of a problem," said the sergeant. "He's seemed to be in pain ever since, but the vets can't say why. He's been X-rayed, and the bone structure is sound. We have a file full of tests that don't say much of anything. There's just a kind of stiffness about him, and he tenses up the minute anyone goes near him with a saddle — he backs away and puts his ears back. No one can ride him." He paused, then added quietly, "Not even me."

Amy looked at him quickly. It was the first time the sergeant had given any indication of his feelings or of his attachment to Venture. But his face was still calm and gave nothing away. "Are you riding a different horse on duty now?" she asked.

Mark shook his head. "We tend to work with one horse at a time. I'm on ordinary station duties until Venture's ready for work again. It's been a good break, but I miss riding."

Amy stared at him. *He misses riding?* she thought. Why wouldn't he say, *"I miss Venture"*? She could feel a tide of emotion welling up. Mark García's description of the storm was vivid and accurate, and yet he somehow seemed detached from it. Suddenly, Amy's heart reached out to Venture, the horse that was still suffering because

GRANT MacEWAN SCHOOL

of that terrible night. *She* knew how deep the damage could go, even if his rider didn't.

"Has Venture received any alternative treatments? Any kind of massage, herbs, anything like that?" asked Lou.

The sergeant shook his head. "No. We take a very straight approach here. But one of the vets had heard of Heartland, and she suggested sending Venture to you."

For an instant, a hint of awkwardness showed in his hazel eyes. Amy read the look in a flash. *This wasn't his idea*, she thought. *He doesn't believe we can help.* Determination flooded through her. She would work with Venture and help to heal the pain that conventional methods couldn't touch.

"May we see Venture led around the yard?" asked Lou, looking over at Amy in an attempt to gauge her reaction.

"Sure," said Sergeant García. "I'll just get a lead rope."

He left Amy and Lou standing by Venture's stall. Lou scratched the horse's neck. "What d'you think, Amy? You've been kind of quiet," she said. "I guess it's tricky when he's had all these examinations already."

"I think we should take him," Amy burst out immediately. "They haven't tried any alternative treatments. There's so much we can do for him." She saw the surprise on Lou's face and composed herself. "But we'll see what he's like when he's led," she added more calmly.

The sergeant walked with long strides across the yard and let himself into Venture's stall. The powerful horse stepped carefully through the door, watching where he placed his hooves, as if he were walking on an unstable surface. Sergeant García led him slowly up the yard and back again.

Amy watched the horse from all angles. There was no obvious problem — no limp, no unevenness in his stride. But there was a definite reluctance in the way he stepped forward, as though he was nervous — but nervousness wasn't quite the right word. As Sergeant García had said, there was a sort of stiffness about him, a hesitancy in his movements, even when he was just walking around his own stable yard.

Amy was curious, and the more she watched the gelding, the more her desire to work with him grew. She looked across at Lou and caught her eye, then gave a determined little nod. Lou looked doubtful but nodded back in agreement.

Amy stepped forward. "I think we could work with Venture at Heartland," she said. She raised her eyes to the sergeant's, challenging him. "If you're sure you think it's worth it," she added.

Sergeant García looked away from her gaze. "That's great," he said. "He deserves all the help he can get."

Lou talked through the arrangements with him. They agreed that Venture should be brought over to Heartland in a couple of days, on Saturday. Rather apologetically, the sergeant pointed out that there was likely to be a lot of media interest and possibly even a local television crew to film Venture's arrival.

"As long as they understand that we're a stable, not a zoo," said Lou. "And that the horses must be treated with respect."

"They're used to that from coming here," the sergeant assured her. "You don't have to worry."

With everything arranged, Amy and Lou climbed into the car and headed back to Heartland.

"I don't think the publicity can really do any harm, do you?" asked Amy.

"Well, like I said, we'll just need to make sure they approach things professionally," said Lou. "I hope they don't come pestering us on a regular basis."

"We had to deal with them before, when we had Gallant Prince," Amy pointed out. "It wasn't too bad then."

"True," agreed Lou. "But we managed to treat him successfully, remember? That made a difference."

"Well, I think we'll have success with Venture, too," said Amy. "I'll make sure we do."

❧

At school the next day, Amy decided to use her lunch hour to learn more about police horses and their training, hoping it would give her useful insights into Venture's problems. To her astonishment, her online search quickly brought up more than she had bargained for. There was a whole series of articles about Sergeant García and Venture, all much more dramatic than the brief account she had seen in the newspaper article Lou had shared. POLICE HORSE CRIPPLED FOR LIFE, ran one headline. NOTHING VENTURED, NOTHING GAINED — POLICE OFFICER SACRIFICES HORSE TO SAVE LOCAL BOYS, read another.

Amy skimmed through the articles. She was appalled at how much some of them twisted the truth. Of course, she had only heard the sergeant's account, but she felt his story seemed honest and forthright. According to one of the online sites, the sergeant had ridden Venture at the car and had managed to get the horse to kick the car door open to free the boys. It was crazy! With a sinking feeling in her stomach, Amy realized that media attention wasn't the problem for Heartland. It was what was actually printed and reported. If reporters started overdramatizing the work they did or got their facts wrong, it could damage Heartland's reputation.

Amy took a deep breath. Venture was going to be a big challenge, but she was still certain that she had made the right decision. She thought once more of his big, noble features and pictured in her mind's eye the terrible moment when the tires had crashed down on his back. If anyone could help a survivor of that night, it would be she and Ty, at Heartland.

℮

After they got back to Heartland, Amy took Molly out for another join-up session. The late afternoon was bright and crisp, ideal for working in the training rings. As she led the mare out, Ben crossed the yard toward her, carrying Red's tack.

"Hi, Ben," Amy greeted him. "Did you just finish?"

Ben nodded. "Yeah. Red did really well today, so we stopped early."

"Did Ty talk to you about next week?" asked Amy, eager to soothe the tension that still lingered between them. "It's fine for you to take some time off."

"Yes, he did, thanks," said Ben.

"That's good," said Amy. She looked at the tall, blond-haired stable hand, standing with the saddle propped on his hip, and wondered if she should say something more — something about how much she appreciated how generous he had been over the past months. Ben did so much yard work, and they would never be able to exercise all the horses without him. But he didn't really do much on the treatment side. Amy wondered if he would like to be more involved in those aspects of the work.

"I'm about to join up with Molly," she said. "Feel like helping me? It would be good for her."

Ben hesitated, then shook his head. "Thanks, Amy,"

he said. "I think I'm better off leaving all that stuff to you and Ty. And I need to clean Red's tack."

"Oh, OK," said Amy. "See you later."

As she led Molly away, she couldn't help feeling frustrated. She didn't know how anyone could refuse a chance to try join up. She wondered guiltily whether it was somehow her fault. Perhaps they should have involved Ben in the treatment side earlier. But at least the offer had been made now. What more could she do than that?

Chapter Four

❧

"Amy! Those are for the reporters!" exclaimed Lou as her sister reached for a chocolate chip cookie.

Amy stepped back from the plate of cookies on the kitchen table and looked at her sister in surprise. They didn't usually make that much of a fuss for owners, let alone journalists! They all had far too much to do. "I was only taking one," she protested. "They'll be too busy taking pictures to eat cookies."

It was Saturday morning. Amy had gone inside to get her gloves and found Grandpa drinking coffee in the kitchen while Lou was setting out slices of bread on the kitchen counter.

"Some of them might have traveled a long way," said Lou. "I'm making tea and coffee and some sandwiches for them, too."

Amy stared at her. This was *definitely* more fuss than usual!

"That's very generous of you, Lou," said Grandpa, taking his coffee cup to the sink. He raised an eyebrow. "Are you hoping they'll give a good report of our catering services?"

Lou blushed. "I just think we should try to give a good impression," she said. "Venture's a bigger challenge than we're used to, and we don't want any bad publicity."

"I could ask Nancy to come over a bit earlier to give you a hand," Grandpa offered. "I'm sure she wouldn't mind."

"No, no, it's fine," Lou protested. She started spreading mustard on the slices of bread. "Honestly, Grandpa. It's all under control."

Amy found her gloves and headed for the door. She didn't understand why Lou was in such a state. Horses arrived all the time, often in much worse condition than Venture. As far as Amy was concerned, sandwiches for the journalists were the last thing on her mind. She needed to make sure that Venture's stall was ready.

By eleven o'clock, a handful of reporters had arrived, their cars clogging the driveway. Grandpa soon had a parking system going. Amy and Ty showed them around the front yard. Despite their obvious curiosity about the rest of the stable grounds, Amy refused to take them farther. By the time they had finished, a local TV crew had shown up, too, and the front yard was swarming with people.

Lou came out with a tray of coffee just as Nancy arrived.

"Oh, Lou, let me take that," said the older woman, looking concerned. "You've got better things to do. If I'd known you were going to go to all this trouble, I would have come sooner to help you out."

"We can manage perfectly well," Lou responded, a little sharply. "Thanks all the same."

Amy took a mug of coffee from the tray for one of the journalists, hearing the sound of a trailer coming up the driveway as she did so. "I think that's Venture," she said.

The trailer rattled up to the front stable block, with Mark García right behind in his car. He parked and jumped out to shake Amy's hand. "Good to see you again," he said. "I see the paparazzi have shown up for our local celebrity."

The sergeant seemed more relaxed away from the police stables, and Amy laughed. "Yes, but they've all been very well behaved," she said. She beckoned to Ty. "Mark, this is Ty Baldwin. He'll be working with Venture, too."

The sergeant smiled and shook Ty's hand. "I bet you'd like to get rid of all these journalists as soon as possible," he said understandingly. "Should we unload Venture right away and let them get their pictures?"

Ty helped Mark undo the bolts on the box, then allowed him to lead out the horse alone. Amy sympathized with the gelding — despite his rigorous training, he was clearly nervous, and he flinched at the barrage of flashes that greeted him at the top of the ramp. Sergeant García urged the horse forward gently as he took small, tentative steps down onto the yard, then past the wall of journalists. Amy showed him Venture's stall and breathed a sigh of relief when the horse was safely inside, away from the snapping cameras.

Sergeant García took off Venture's halter and joined Amy outside the stall to answer questions. They all seemed to come at once.

"What can Heartland offer that police vets can't?"

"How long will you be keeping him here?"

"Sergeant García, can you turn this way, please? More to the left," called a TV cameraman.

Amy found herself explaining and re-explaining the work that went on at Heartland, hoping desperately that she was making it clear enough, while Sergeant García answered questions about the night of the storm and Venture's injuries. It was exhausting. Amy felt like snapping at the reporters several times when they asked questions she'd already answered, but she followed the sergeant's lead, smiling and nodding, until at last it was over.

"Hope that was bearable for you," said the sergeant when the last journalist had climbed into her car and driven off. "It won't be so bad from now on. Don't be afraid to tell them there's nothing to report."

Now that the barrage of questions was over, Amy felt impressed with the sergeant's calm, professional approach. It had helped a lot. He still seemed cool and detached, but Amy could see how his demeanor was an asset in a stressful situation.

Amy slid the bolt open and let herself into Venture's stall. The sergeant leaned over the half door and stroked Venture's ears, watching as Amy put a few drops of Rescue Remedy in his water.

"What's that?" he asked.

Amy looked up at him. She guessed he didn't think much of these sorts of remedies, but his curiosity seemed genuine enough. She smiled.

"Bach Rescue Remedy. It's good for sudden change and shock," she explained. "We always give it to new arrivals, to help them settle in." The police horse nosed his water and took a few gulps. "Horses tend to know what's good for them," she said. "That's one of the principles we stand by." She threw the police sergeant another glance, wondering how he'd respond.

Sergeant García shrugged. "Well, I'm sure you'll do your best for him. I'm going to miss him." He stood at the stall door, seeming at a loss. "I'd best get going," he said eventually.

Amy took him to say good-bye to Ty and Lou, then walked with him toward his car.

"Bye, Amy. I'll be in touch very soon," he said.

"We'll let you know if there's any progress," Amy promised. "Please feel free to drop by anytime."

Mark climbed into his car, and Amy watched as he put his key in the ignition. He seemed to be taking his time about it. She wondered if there was something wrong and was about to step forward when she saw him swat a fly away from his face. She decided it was fine to head back to the house. She was halfway to the door when a sudden realization hit her.

He hadn't been swatting a fly. He'd been wiping away a tear.

In the kitchen, Lou and Nancy had almost finished clearing away the dishes. Amy poured herself the dregs from the coffeepot and wandered into the den for a moment, lost in thought. Had she imagined it? Calm, professional Sergeant García? She ran the scene through her mind's eye again. No, she was right. She had seen the glistening tear on his cheek before he brushed it away.

She went back into the kitchen and placed her mug in the sink, then went out to Venture's stall. He was standing quietly in the darkness at the back and shifted nervously when she unbolted the half door and stepped inside.

"Hello there, boy," she said. "It's OK. I'm just going to stroke you to make you feel a bit better."

Slowly, so as not to startle him, she reached out and touched his withers, then began to gently massage the area with little circling movements of her fingertips. Venture instantly tensed up. Amy kept on going, moving the circles from his withers up his neck and murmuring to him, but the more she continued to touch him, the more agitated he became. Suddenly, he shifted away from her, and with a jolt of surprise Amy saw fear in the whites of his eyes.

Patiently, she tried again. It was very rare for a horse not to respond to T-touch. She was sure that if she could just keep going steadily for a few moments, he would begin to relax a little. But Venture wouldn't allow it, and Amy began to see telltale warning signs that he might be about to react more aggressively: There was growing tension in his neck, and his ears were flattened back. Amy stepped away. There was no point in pushing it.

A shadow fell across the door. It was Ty. "He's one unhappy horse, isn't he?"

Amy nodded. "I can't remember the last horse that wouldn't respond to T-touch," she said. "Maybe we should let him settle down a bit longer and give the Rescue Remedy more time to take effect."

"We could give him some Star of Bethlehem, too," suggested Ty. "His trauma from the accident obviously goes pretty deep. It'll help to lift the sense of shock."

Amy looked at Ty, and their eyes locked. They didn't need to say it, but they both knew all about the long-lasting effects of that night. She leaned her head against the horse's strong, muscled neck, a lump rising in her throat.

"Good idea," she managed to say. "We have to help him somehow, Ty."

"We will," said Ty softly. He let himself into the stall and touched Amy's arm. "Remember all the hours you spent sitting by my bedside, talking to me. And all the hours you spent helping me after I'd come around. How many times did I drop a fork and you picked it up? I know it must have been trying, Amy. I don't know how you found the strength to believe I'd make it. But you did. You were with me for every small step, and now I'm here."

Amy nodded and scrubbed at her face with her sleeve. Ty reached up and laid his hand on the police horse's neck. "So I know you'll pull through for Venture, too," he finished. "And this time, I'm right by your side."

After lunch, Amy and Ty went down to the paddocks together to catch Dazzle. For once, there was time for the two of them to go on a trail ride.

Amy watched from the gate as Ty approached the mustang with a halter. She loved watching them work together. When he was being caught, Dazzle was always torn between his love of freedom and his desire to be with Ty, and it could take several minutes for him to allow Ty to put on the halter. Ty walked toward him slowly, then turned away as though he had lost interest. Dazzle kept on grazing, but Amy could see that he still had his eye on Ty. Gradually, they inched closer until Dazzle submitted and allowed himself to be caught.

"He's a real tease, isn't he?" Amy said with a laugh as Ty led the stallion to the gate.

Ty nodded ruefully. "Yeah. But he's never spiteful. He just likes the game."

They led the stallion up to the front yard. Amy let Ty go on ahead while she got her own pony, Sundance, from the barn. Sundance, usually so grumpy with other horses, seemed to take to Dazzle. Amy thought it was because he accepted the stallion as leader, so he didn't make his usual sneaky attempts to assert himself. Whatever the reason, taking Sundance on a trail ride with Dazzle was a pleasure.

They set off up the track toward Clairdale Ridge, with Dazzle slightly in front. Both horses were enjoying the bright February afternoon, arching their necks and skittering over the hard ground — especially Sundance, who was kept indoors more over the winter. Ty pushed Dazzle into a trot, and they soon reached the open ground where they could canter. Since Ty was still schooling Dazzle and getting him accustomed to working outside of the ring, they cantered along very sedately, with Amy and Sundance setting the pace. It was a calming ride, and as they slowed to a trot, Amy found herself wishing that she and Ty could have more times like this. If only they could keep Dazzle!

But then she pushed the thought away. There were always new horses to ride at Heartland, and Dazzle wasn't the first that Ty had grown close to. Accepting that things moved on and embracing new challenges as they arrived was a vital part of what they did. They bonded with horses, then had to let them go.

Thinking about this reminded Amy of Ben. Red was the only horse that he had a strong bond with; he wasn't interested in developing that kind of bond with any of the others. She turned in her saddle and waited for Ty to ride up next to her.

"Ben seems really worked up about this show," she commented. "Even more than usual. I get this feeling there's something on his mind."

"I guess Brideswell is a big event," said Ty. "Since the flu knocked them out of the running last year, I think Ben really wants to qualify early in the season."

"Even so . . ." Amy trailed off and stroked Sundance's neck, thinking how exciting it would be for Ben and Red to go to the jumper finals. "He didn't want to join up with Molly," she said. "He's just so preoccupied. Like he can't concentrate on Heartland at all."

Ty opened his mouth to say something, then seemed to change his mind. "Well, he'll always put Red first," he said. "I don't think we're ever going to change that."

"No," Amy agreed uncomfortably. "I guess not."

Amy didn't want the ride to end, but all too soon they were clattering back into the yard. Ty untacked Dazzle and took him down to the paddock while Amy settled Sundance in his stall. She was still thinking about Ben. Perhaps she needed to give him more space to be the person he wanted to be. If she didn't accept him as he was — his goals and priorities — things were always going to be difficult.

She picked up a grooming kit to give Sundance a rubdown and was soon absorbed in giving his buckskin coat long, smooth sweeps with the body brush.

A voice interrupted her and she looked up. It was Ben.

"Hi, Amy," he greeted her. He seemed uneasy. "Are you busy?"

Amy gave Sundance's mane a few quick strokes. "Well, just the usual," she said. "Why? Is something wrong?"

"No, not really," said Ben. "It's just that . . ." He trailed off and Amy stopped brushing.

"Just what?" she asked gently. "Are you OK?"

"Yes. Yes, I'm fine," said Ben. He took a deep breath. "It's just that I'm thinking of leaving Heartland," he finished in a rush.

Amy dropped the body brush and stared at him.

"Leaving?" she echoed, dumbfounded.

Ben nodded, his blue eyes troubled. "I'm sorry, Amy. I've been thinking it over for weeks. It's not that I don't like the work here or what you do. It's all fantastic and I've learned a lot. You and Ty are both amazing. But it's just not for me. I've realized I want to concentrate on competing. To really give it all my energy."

Amy couldn't quite take it in. "Leaving," she said again, almost in wonderment. Ben looked at her awkwardly.

"So when are you planning on going?" Amy asked.

"I don't have anything lined up yet," Ben admitted. "I wanted to talk to you first. But I'm going to start looking for a place at a competition yard. That'll be the best way to maximize Red's potential. I really owe it to him, Amy. He could make it to the top, but I can't spend enough time with him here."

Amy felt something twist inside her. She thought of how she had given up competing on her own horse, Storm, because she wanted to put Heartland first — but here was Ben, walking away from it all. She forced a smile. "Well. It must have been a difficult decision to make," she managed to say. "I'll be sorry to see you go, Ben. Really sorry. But I guess you have to do what's right for you."

Ben nodded. "Yeah. I'll miss you guys, and everything here, believe me. I just think that the time has come to move on."

Amy picked up the body brush, trying to push down her feelings. Part of her wanted to beg Ben to stay. They needed him. Things were just getting back to normal. But, instead, she smiled again. "Well, I hope you find a good yard," she said. "You're right, you know, you and Red could go all the way to the top."

Ben looked relieved. "Thanks for being so understanding, Amy," he said. "But you're not getting rid of me quite so fast. It might take a while to find the right place, and anyway, I won't go until you've found someone to replace me. If you decide to, that is."

Amy couldn't bring herself to think that far. "Well, we can talk about that later," she said.

Ben nodded and headed off. Amy quickly finished up with Sundance, her mind reeling, then took the grooming kit back to the tack room. Ty was in there, giving Dazzle's tack a quick wipe. He looked up as she came in.

"What's up?" he asked immediately. "Is it Venture?"

Amy felt herself welling up. "Ben just told me he's leaving," she said, feeling a tear roll down her cheek. "I can't believe it."

Ty stood up and put his arms around her. "He was so worried about telling you," he said. "I'm glad he finally did."

Amy stepped back sharply. "You *knew*?" she exclaimed. "You knew, and you didn't tell me! Ty! How *could* you?"

"Ben asked me not to," Ty said simply. "He wanted to tell you himself — when he was ready."

"But he told *you*." Amy slumped down on one of the tack trunks, feeling almost winded — and somehow betrayed. She stared at the wooden floor.

"Hey," Ty said softly. "It's not the way you think it is. Ben knew you'd take it hard. That's why he wanted to be sure before he said anything to you."

Amy looked up and searched Ty's face. His eyes were full of warmth and concern. He held out a hand and pulled her to her feet.

"Don't feel bad," he said, gazing into her eyes. "You've still got me, right?"

Amy nodded, trying to stem the tears that were now flowing freely. "I just can't believe it," she said in a strangled voice. "I — I knew something was wrong, but I never thought . . . Ty, is it my fault?"

Ty looked startled. "*Your* fault? Why on earth would you think that?"

Amy bowed her head. Ty drew her close to him and kissed the top of her head. "People move on, just like horses, Amy," he whispered. "That's what Heartland's about, remember? As long as we stay true to that, everything else can change."

❧

By the next morning, Amy felt a bit better. It was Sunday, and there was no rush to get ready for school, so she decided to put off her morning session with Molly until later in the day. She was leading the mare out of her stall when she heard a car coming up the driveway. She paused, curious. They weren't expecting anyone. Surely it wasn't a reporter, anticipating an update on Venture already!

The car pulled into the yard, and a woman in her midtwenties jumped out. She was small and slender, with long blond hair and pale features. She approached Amy with a big smile, and Molly gave a whinny of welcome.

Amy realized that this must be Eloise Beatson, Molly's owner. "Hello," she greeted her. "I'm Amy Fleming. You must be . . ."

"Eloise." The woman smiled. "It's good to meet you." She put her arm around Molly's neck and gave her a hug.

Molly nudged Eloise with her nose, her ears pricked. Amy was intrigued to see the mare's happy response to her owner. It was hard to believe that they had any problems at all. "She sure is pleased to see you," she laughed.

Eloise nodded. "I miss her so much. I was passing by, so I thought I'd drop in to see how she's doing."

"I was just about to take her to the training ring," said Amy. "Would you like to come and watch?"

Eloise willingly agreed. Amy handed her the lead rope and watched as horse and owner walked just ahead of her down the track. She wasn't sure if she was just imagining it, but Molly seemed slightly more nervous today. The mare was jogging and tugging on the lead rope, which she didn't do when Amy was walking with her. It could be Molly's excitement at seeing Eloise again — but it might be something else.

She caught up with Eloise to walk alongside her. Molly was showing other signs of mild nerves, and Amy realized she was right. The mare *was* pleased to see her owner — but she was definitely somewhat agitated, too.

"Has she been acting up with you?" asked Eloise.

"Not so far," said Amy. "But I haven't been riding her, I've just been working with her from the ground. I want to make sure she trusts me before I go any further."

Eloise sighed. "I was afraid that would happen," she said.

Amy was puzzled. "What d'you mean?"

"I didn't think she'd give you any problems," said Eloise. Her almond-colored eyes looked disenchanted. "I think she blames me for the accident, so she's punishing me. She's been fine with everyone else."

Amy shook her head. "Horses aren't naturally vindictive," she said. "And Molly's one of the most affectionate horses I've come across. She wouldn't hold a grudge like that. But a horse can lose its trust in its rider or owner. Have you ever seen join up?"

Eloise shook her head, so Amy explained why it was an essential part of Molly's treatment. "When horses are ridden, they place their trust in their rider. They are basically fight-or-flight creatures, so their instinct is to protect their hooves and legs at all costs. They won't step into something they can't see clearly, like muddy water or long grass, unless they're sure it's safe. But a trusting horse will do it if his rider asks him to."

"That's just what I said. Molly resents me for taking her through that creek," said Eloise.

"It's not resentment," said Amy carefully. "It's more that she needs reassurance. She's very trusting by nature, so her accident was a big blow to her confidence. She doubts her own judgment as much as she doubts yours."

Eloise looked uncertain. "Well, I guess that makes sense," she said. "So you're using join up to teach her to trust again?"

"That's right," said Amy. "I'll join up with her first, then it would be a good idea if you did it, too."

She took the lead rope from Eloise and unclipped it, then drove the horse away from her around the ring. Eloise retreated to the gate as Amy pushed Molly into making the well-practiced choice: to stay on the rail or come to the center of the ring to be with her.

"Your turn now," said Amy, walking to the gate with Molly close behind her. She hoisted herself onto the fence to watch. "First of all, you have to make yourself the aggressor," she told Eloise. "Stand tall, drive her away from you with exaggerated motions, and then make sure to keep her moving."

Eloise began to do as Amy said, but without much conviction. Her body language was tentative, and she only took a few short steps toward the horse. Molly was unsure what Eloise wanted and simply lowered her head to blow in the dust.

"Really drive her," Amy encouraged. "Use your arms to shoo her away."

Eloise strode more confidently toward her horse. Molly threw up her head and backed off. Eloise stopped. "I can't," she called, biting her lip. "How can it be right to drive her away? She might not come back."

"She will," Amy promised. She jumped down from the fence and went to stand beside Eloise. But as she got closer, she realized to her alarm that the young woman was close to tears.

"She'll come back to you. She won't to me. You're the one who said she doesn't trust me," said Eloise in a trembling voice. "I can't send her away. I really can't."

Suddenly, Amy realized that it wasn't only Molly's confidence that had been threatened. It was Eloise's, too. The problem wasn't quite as simple as Amy had thought. She could help Molly to regain her confidence, but unless Eloise regained hers as well, they'd soon be back where they started.

Chapter Five

"I think it would help if you could drop by whenever you have the chance," Amy told Eloise as they walked back to her car. Amy had taken over join up in order to leave Molly with a sense of trust — but her renewed faith was not in Eloise.

"Do you think that will help?" asked Eloise.

"Yes," said Amy firmly. "It's important that we work with Molly together. We'll start by having her walk over poles and such, then, as she improves, we'll try her over puddles and other troublesome surfaces. As she takes on new challenges, her trust in herself and others will grow."

Eloise smiled, still looking a little pale. "I hope so, Amy," she said. "I think you're doing a great job. I don't want to mess it all up."

"She's your horse," Amy reminded her gently. "It's your relationship with her that we need to put back on track. But we'll get there, I promise."

Eloise drove off, and Amy went inside for Sunday brunch. Lou and Ty were already sitting at the table, while Nancy was helping Grandpa serve scrambled eggs and fried tomatoes. Ben had gone to have lunch with his mother, which made it easier to talk about his departure. It had come as a shock to everyone.

"I'll put an ad in the local paper for a replacement," said Lou, pouring more coffee. "And on our Web site as well. We'll probably get the most responses that way."

"Good idea," agreed Jack. "But I don't imagine we'll be short of applicants."

Amy sat down, suddenly feeling sad again. Ben had been through so much with them all. How could he just walk away?

"You're going to be busy, Lou," said Nancy, handing around slices of toast. "It's not going to be easy, making wedding plans on top of recruiting new staff."

Amy looked at Lou with a jolt, remembering that she, too, would be leaving when she got married. She felt as though the legs on her chair had given way. Everyone was abandoning Heartland!

"I'm sure I'll cope," said Lou politely.

"Oh, yes," said Nancy. "You're very capable. But I'm

sure you'll appreciate some help, just the same. I've been thinking — I'd love to make your wedding cake for you. That would be one thing off your list, wouldn't it?"

Lou frowned. "It's a bit soon to be thinking about that, isn't it?" she began.

"Oh, no," insisted Nancy. "It's much better to plan things early. I've brought some books for you to look at. You'll want to choose the recipe yourself, I'm sure. Most brides do."

Lou took a deep breath. "Thank you, Nancy," she said, clearly trying her best to be gracious. "I'll take a look when I've got a minute."

Amy realized she'd been holding her breath and let it out with relief. For the time being, it looked as though Lou was still concentrating on Heartland. Right now, Amy didn't want to face the thought of her sister's mind turning elsewhere.

When Amy got on the school bus the next morning, it felt as though a week had passed, not a weekend. So much had happened — Venture's arrival, Eloise's session with Molly, but above all, Ben's announcement. As Amy sat down next to Soraya, she wondered how her friend would react. She had liked Ben before she started dating Matt.

Soraya launched into telling Amy about her weekend — how she and Matt had gone to the movies, how they'd eaten too much ice cream, how they'd walked through the woods on Sunday and thought they'd gotten lost.

At last her recounting came to an end. "So how was your weekend?" she asked.

Amy looked Soraya in the eyes. "Ben's leaving," she told her.

Soraya gave a little gasp. "*Leaving!*" she exclaimed. "Amy! But . . . why?"

"He wants to move to a competition yard," Amy replied, "so he can concentrate on jumping."

Soraya recovered and looked thoughtful. "Well, I guess that makes sense," she said matter-of-factly. "Red always meant more to him than anything else. Are you going to hire someone else?"

"Lou's putting an ad on our Web site," said Amy.

"I bet you'll get tons of responses," said Soraya. "A lot of people would love to work somewhere like Heartland."

Amy nodded, feeling a little flat. Soraya was taking the news in stride. Everyone seemed to think it was the obvious thing for him to do. Why was Amy the only one who wasn't ready to see him go?

❦

It was a relief to leave school behind and get back to Heartland. Over the next few days, Amy concentrated on Molly and Venture. Join up progressed quickly with Molly, and Amy was soon able to start riding her. At first, the mare was nervous, sidestepping and running backward whenever she encountered something new. But the join-up sessions had done their work. With a little reassurance and encouragement, the mare began to put her trust in Amy, and she soon started walking across different surfaces without a problem — through muddy patches, areas strewn with straw, or on a narrow path in between logs.

One evening, Eloise visited again. She was delighted to hear how well the mare had been doing, but Amy could tell that the news of the horse's progress did not bolster her owner's confidence. As they led Molly down to the training ring, Amy encouraged Eloise to try join up again.

"I promise she'll respond," Amy reassured her. "Just trust in the process. She'll want to join you in the middle of the ring as soon as you let her."

"Well, if you're really sure," said Eloise reluctantly.

"I'm certain of it," said Amy emphatically.

She opened the gate and led the mare into the ring. After showing Eloise how far the mare had progressed with different obstacles, she handed Eloise the lead rope. "She's all yours," she said with a grin, backing away toward the gate.

Amy watched as Eloise took a deep breath, then unclipped the lead rope and drove the mare away from her around the ring. Amy knew Eloise needed to have success. Her relationship with Molly depended on it.

"Keep her going for a while, until she's giving really clear signals," called Amy.

Eloise gave a determined little nod. She drove Molly on until she was chewing fervently, pleading to be allowed to join her owner. Then, when Eloise slowly turned her back, Molly didn't hesitate. The mare walked over at once to nuzzle her shoulder and blow gently in her hair. Eloise's face was pure joy, and Amy smiled to herself. It was great to see this horse and rider team gradually rebuilding their faith in each other.

But work with Venture was not progressing as smoothly. It was difficult to do active work with him. Movement of any kind caused him pain and distress, so join up was out of the question. Amy had decided to try a mixture of Bach Flower treatments and massage to reach the horse, but even that wasn't working. He still seemed to hate T-touch, which Amy found baffling. She couldn't imagine that it would be causing him pain. It was such a gentle technique.

"It's almost as if he's hurting all over," Amy commented one evening as she and Ty led the police horse slowly down the track for some exercise. "That makes it hard to find the source of the pain."

"Yes — and his being depressed doesn't help, either," agreed Ty, as Venture came to a halt several steps behind them.

"Come on, Venture," encouraged Amy, realizing that he had stopped walking altogether.

Venture hung his head and didn't move. When Amy tugged on his lead rope, he simply stretched out his neck, as if that was all the energy he could muster. Ty gave the horse an encouraging nudge from behind and, very reluctantly, Venture stepped forward again.

"I wonder if there's something that all those experts missed," Amy said worriedly. "Something physical, I mean. It's just not normal for him to hate exercise so much, is it? It'd be awful if we were causing more damage."

"We could get Scott to give him another check," suggested Ty. "But like you say, he's had so many examinations already. It's very strange."

They coaxed the horse around one of the paddocks, knowing he would develop other health problems if he stopped moving altogether, then led him back to his stall. Leaving Ty to give him a gentle rubdown, Amy went inside to phone Scott. The sooner the vet came over, the better.

❧

"Do you want to talk to Scott?" Amy asked Lou, picking up the phone. "I'm about to call him."

Lou looked up from the pile of job applications in front of her. "Oh? What about?"

Amy hesitated. "Venture," she said reluctantly. Her sister's doubts about the horse seemed to be growing with each day that passed, and Amy didn't like to admit there wasn't any improvement.

Lou looked concerned. "Amy, Scott's a wonderful vet, but he's not a miracle worker. Venture's already been seen by every specialist under the sun."

"I know, I know," said Amy hurriedly. "I just want him to give his back another once-over, that's all."

Lou pursed her lips and frowned. "You know, there's one reporter who just won't go away," she said. "She phones almost every day. I keep putting her off, but it would be nice to have some good news to pass on."

"It's going to take time. Sergeant García said we shouldn't worry about the media," Amy replied in a slightly defensive tone. "Do you want to speak to Scott when I'm done or not?"

Lou shook her head, then turned back to the applications. Quickly, Amy punched in the vet's number and asked him to come over as soon as he could so that they could redirect Venture's treatment if necessary. When she'd finished, Lou had clearly decided to drop the Venture discussion, because she looked up with a smile.

"We've had quite a few responses to our ad," she said. "Want to take a look?"

"Sure!" said Amy, feeling relieved. "Does anyone have real potential?"

"I think so."

Amy sat down next to Lou as she flicked through the applications. There were seven altogether.

"I think these two girls are probably too inexperienced," said Lou, handing Amy the printouts. "Neither of them has actually worked with horses before. They've done a bit of riding. Both are horse crazy, of course."

Amy smiled and scanned their applications. "It's a shame," she said. "But you're right, we need someone who knows what she's doing, at least in terms of stable management."

Lou handed Amy the rest of the papers. "The others all seem like they might be OK," she said. "Take a look."

Amy perused them quickly. There was Jay, who had been a groom and exercise boy at a racing stable; Patrick, now retired, who was probably the most experienced of all, having spent his life working with horses; Joni, whose parents ran a Morgan stud farm in Alberta, Canada; Stephanie, who had three years' experience working at a riding stable; and Zoë, who owned a dressage horse.

"She'd be looking to stable him here," Lou pointed out.

"Well, that's OK," said Amy. "We stable Red without a problem. It would be good to meet her."

"What about the others?" asked Lou.

Amy spent a few minutes reading. "I'm not sure about Patrick," she said after a while. "He's experienced, sure. But I'm not certain he'd fit in here. He talks about breaking horses instead of gentling or backing them. It's not a good sign. If he had any real understanding of places like Heartland, he'd know that we think differently. After all, we've been in the papers more than once by now."

Lou's face clouded over at the mention of newspapers and Amy quickly moved on. She scanned the rest of the applications. "I think it would be good to meet everyone else, though. They all sound like they might fit in. It's so difficult to tell by just reading about them."

"So that's Jay, Stephanie, Joni, and Zoë," said Lou. "We should discuss it with Ty and Grandpa, then I'll set up some interviews."

"Ty's mom is picking him up early tonight," said Amy. "Maybe we could talk about it over supper tomorrow?"

"Good plan," said Lou. "I'll ask Grandpa if that's OK."

❧

"See you later!" Amy called to Ty and Ben the next morning, heading inside for her shower.

It had been a rush to get everything done, as usual. Amy had spent half an hour with Venture. Her hands were aching after massaging his neck over and over with diluted lavender oil, but the police horse still wouldn't respond. Amy was relieved that Scott had said he would come sometime that day. She hoped he'd be able to offer some reassurance about Venture's physical condition, at least.

She rushed into the shower. Ten minutes later she was bounding down the stairs, her long brown hair still damp.

"Do you want a ride home from school tonight?" asked Lou, as Amy grabbed her coat. "I have to go to the grocery store. I can pick you up, if you like."

"Great," said Amy, wrapping her scarf around her neck. "See you then."

The day dragged. Amy was impatient to know what Ty and Grandpa would make of the job applications and anxious to hear what Scott would say about Venture. She drifted in and out of her own thoughts and wondered if schoolwork would ever really matter to her as much as it was supposed to. Only rarely, when it was about something that really interested her, such as the environment, did it take over from her thoughts about Heartland.

At last the final bell rang and she was able to head to the school parking lot to find Lou.

"I've already done the shopping," Lou told her. "Scott called just as I was leaving. He was running late, but he should be at Heartland by the time we get back." She glanced sideways at Amy and smiled. "He's staying for supper."

Amy glanced at the ring on her sister's finger. In some ways, their engagement made no difference at all; Lou and Scott were both so busy that they had little chance to see much of each other. But that would change once they were married.

"That journalist called again today," Lou went on, her voice becoming anxious. "I'm running out of things to say."

"They can't expect us to work a miracle in five minutes. I mean, the police vets were on the case for weeks!" Amy exclaimed. "I'm not going to give up on Venture just because a few journalists keep pestering us, Lou. Think of Ty. We didn't give up on him after the storm, did we?"

"I wasn't suggesting you give up on him," Lou responded quietly. "I just worry, that's all."

Amy lapsed into silence. She knew that Lou was right to be concerned — if only for Venture's sake. They had so little to go on, but Amy felt invested in the police horse. She knew it was up to them to help him through.

And while she didn't like to admit it, the constant media pressure was beginning to get to her, too.

Scott's pickup was parked in the driveway when they arrived. Amy helped Lou unload the groceries and staggered into the kitchen with her hands full of bags, Lou just behind her. Scott and Nancy were sitting at the table.

"Hi, girls!" said Nancy as they dumped the bags on the kitchen floor. "Do you need some help?"

"No, thanks, that's it," said Lou. "What are you two up to?"

Scott looked up and grinned. "Wedding stationery," he said, blushing just a bit. "Nancy's been introducing me to all the different options. It's intriguing — there's so much to choose from."

The smile died on Lou's lips. "Oh," she said, leaning down to unpack the grocery bags. "Well, could you move that stuff off the table, please? It's covering up the job applications. We have to review those at supper."

Amy saw Scott's face cloud with disappointment. Nancy gave Lou a puzzled look. "If I didn't know any better, I'd think you didn't want to get married, Lou!" she quipped.

Lou straightened up quickly. "That's not true," she retorted. "I just . . ." She stopped, twisting a can of chopped tomatoes in her hands.

"Wedding nerves," said Nancy knowingly. "Happens to everyone."

Lou's eyes flashed open, and she glared at Nancy for a full five seconds before turning away and shuffling through the last of the canned goods. Lou kept her back to everyone as she noisily stacked tuna and soup on the shelves. For a heart-stopping moment, Amy wondered if her sister was getting cold feet about the engagement.

Scott got to his feet. "Hey, Lou," he said quietly. "No worries. We don't have to rush into anything. We can take our time making up our minds."

He touched her arm and Lou relaxed. "Sorry," she muttered, resting her head on Scott's shoulder for an instant. Amy saw him smile down at her and realized there was nothing wrong between them, so she had no idea why Lou had gotten so upset.

"I'll clear everything out of your way," said Nancy. "I need to get going, anyway." She gathered together the stationery samples and made room for them in her bag.

"Aren't you staying for supper?" asked Amy as Nancy shrugged on her thick woolen coat. "Grandpa should be back from the feed market soon."

"No, I was just dropping by with those samples," said Nancy. "I need to get back home. I'm cooking dinner for an old friend of mine. But thanks anyway. Don't forget to take a look at those cake recipes, Lou!" She gave a quick wave at the door and was gone.

Lou took the toilet paper and shampoo off the counter

and disappeared into the bathroom. When she came back, she was her usual composed self.

"I'm ready to take a look at Venture when you are, Amy," said Scott when they'd finished with the groceries.

"Sure," Amy replied, heading for the door.

They found the police horse standing at the back of his stall, his head drooping. Amy slipped a halter over his head, then led him slowly toward the paddock. Venture took small, reluctant steps, resisting Amy as she gently pulled on the lead rope.

Scott scrutinized the horse from all angles, then gave him a thorough physical examination, working his way carefully all over his body. When he'd finished, the vet shook his head. "I really can't find anything wrong with him. There's no inflammation or swelling in any of the joints. There might be an underlying back problem, but he's had X rays, and the police would have brought in experts to check him out. If they didn't find anything . . ." He shrugged.

Amy stroked Venture's nose. She couldn't bear to watch his suffering, not knowing what to try next. "We're using different flower remedies," she told Scott. "Star of Bethlehem for the original shock of the accident and Rock Rose to help lift his fear of pain. Ty and I had the idea that the memory of pain can be as bad as the pain itself. So I keep trying to massage him to help him relax, but I can't tell if it's doing much. He hates T-touch, so I just give him a short lavender oil massage every day to release the tension."

Scott nodded. "Sounds good. Your theory about his recalling his pain may have some merit. But keep looking for physical clues, too. Slight changes might indicate what the real problem is."

Scott headed back to the house. Amy watched him go, feeling frustrated. It felt like all the treatments were no better than a shot in the dark. Many of Heartland's methods required a long time to take effect, but she hadn't seen a single positive sign. Amy thought of Lou's concerns. She wasn't ready to admit defeat with Venture yet — especially not to the press.

After putting the horse away, Amy went down to the training ring where Ty was schooling Dazzle. His owners, Mr. and Mrs. Abrahams, wanted to be able to ride him, but they weren't experienced enough to train him themselves. Amy smiled as she approached the gate. Ty's work was having great results — the stallion was turning into a reliable and responsive riding horse.

This evening, Ty was teaching him how to back up. Amy helped by pushing gently on his shoulders as Ty gave the aids so that Dazzle understood what was being asked of him. By the end of the session, the stallion had willingly taken four steps backward in a straight line — a major achievement! Feeling grateful for this sign of success, Amy and Ty turned Dazzle into his field and wandered up to the farmhouse for supper.

Ben and Scott were already sitting at the table chatting about Ben's plans as they walked in, while Jack washed his hands at the sink.

Lou was taking pizza out of the oven. "Have a seat," she said. "I'm just about to serve everyone."

"Looks great," said Ty hungrily.

"Well, dig in," said Lou, handing out plates. "We'll look at the applications afterward. You don't have to stick around for that, Ben."

Amy looked across at Ben unhappily. She hated the idea that he wasn't going to be part of things for much longer — it just didn't seem right.

Ben shifted in his seat. "I don't mind sticking around. I'm sort of interested, to be honest," he said with a slightly shy smile.

Once everyone had eaten their fill of pizza, Lou handed out copies of the applications. Scott got up and made coffee. There was silence for a while, apart from the rustle of paper, as everyone read about the applicants.

"Amy and I had a look earlier," said Lou. "We thought that four of them sounded hopeful — Stephanie, Jay" — she paused to flick through her set of papers — "Joni, and Zoë. We thought the two other girls were too inexperienced, and Patrick was too experienced, in the wrong way. What does everyone else think?"

"I'd agree with that," said Ty. He cast a quick glance at Ben. "The other one I have doubts about is Zoë."

Amy read through Zoë's application again. Her dressage horse, Samurai, featured heavily, and there was a list of the competitions she had won recently. Amy could see Ty's issue. It was obvious that Zoë already had some serious demands on her time. She drew a deep breath. Still, no one had seconded Ty's misgivings.

"Don't worry about offending me," said Ben. "I can see a potential problem with her. She wants to stable her dressage horse here, so she'll probably have other priorities." He paused and looked around the table. "Like me."

Ty looked relieved. "Well, yeah, that's what I was thinking," he admitted. "It might be better to have someone who wants to focus on Heartland, someone who doesn't have other riding goals. What do you think, Amy?"

Amy was glad that Ben had been so frank. She realized it wasn't easy, discussing what they were looking for with him sitting there.

"You're right," she said awkwardly. "I'm glad you noticed it . . . and . . . and thanks for understanding, Ben. We'll go with the other three. Is that OK with you, Grandpa?"

Jack Bartlett nodded and put the papers down. "Yes,

that all sounds good to me," he said. "I'm sure one of them will be just what we're looking for."

To her surprise, as they all put the papers down and started drinking their coffee, Amy suddenly felt a lot better. She looked across at Ben. Now that the discussion was over, he seemed relaxed. It suddenly occurred to her that for him, this wasn't an ending at all. It was a chance at a whole new life and a new focus, and it would be amazing to watch his career develop. Amy was sure he'd go far.

And for Heartland, things were going to change, too. What might a new person bring? Amy realized that this was the sort of change she welcomed. There would be new ideas, new input, a whole new atmosphere.

It was all a new beginning.

Chapter Six

❧

Sundance's ears were pinned flat against his head, and his tail swished testily. He was every inch the picture of a bad-tempered pony — and then some. Amy led him back toward his stall, murmuring to him soothingly as she went.

"Come on, boy, it wasn't that bad," she whispered, stroking his mane.

Sundance flicked his ears and grew calmer. Then he butted Amy affectionately, and she laughed.

"In you go," she said, opening the door of his stall. She led him in and slipped off the halter, watching with a smile as the pony headed straight for his hay net and started snatching at it greedily.

"You did a good job, old boy," she told him softly, and

walked up to the front yard, where Ty was just bringing Stephanie out of the feed room.

It was Saturday morning. Things had been happening fast over the last few days. All three candidates had wanted to schedule an interview for that weekend, and Stephanie had been the first to arrive. She was tall, with long dark hair pulled back off her face and tied in a ponytail.

"We'll let you know very soon," Amy heard Ty say at the feed-room door.

Amy walked over, smiling. "Did you have any other questions?"

Stephanie shook her head. "Not really, but thanks so much for showing me everything. It's really great here," she said. Then she frowned. "I guess you wanted me to spot what the problem is with Sundance. He's a tricky one. Seems like he needs a few good schooling sessions to teach him to respond to commands more promptly. That's what I'd recommend, anyway."

Amy nodded, her eyebrows raised. She hoped her expression didn't give anything away. "Thanks, Stephanie. It's good to hear your ideas," she said. "And thank you for coming. Like Ty said, we'll let you know in the next few days."

Ty walked Stephanie to her car, then came back to find Amy in the tack room, where she was quickly wiping Sundance's bridle. He grinned at her. "A few good schooling sessions!" he echoed. "What happened in the training ring?"

"Well, I thought I'd give her Sundance to ride," explained Amy. "You know how grumpy he can be. I hoped it might show how she deals with difficult horses."

"And?" queried Ty.

"Needless to say, Sundance didn't think much of her. Her response was to tell me he was acting up, then she asked me for a crop." Amy grinned mischievously.

"You didn't give her one, did you?"

"Of course not," said Amy. "I didn't want to be responsible for what Sundance might have done. I just told her to do what she could with him. She got quite frustrated trying to make him canter. He kept bulging to the outside and picking up the wrong lead. She said he needed to be taught a lesson." She frowned. "I don't mind all that — Sundance can be a real brat. It was more that it didn't cross her mind to think of another way of handling the situation or even to ask me what I thought she should do. You'd think that if she'd done her homework about Heartland, she'd be a bit more open-minded."

Ty nodded. "Yeah. To be honest, she didn't seem very interested when I showed her around the feed room. I talked to her about the flower remedies and herbs, but she didn't ask any questions."

Amy sighed. "Oh, well. On to the next one. It's Jay, isn't it? The groom whose old stable is closing down?"

"Yes, and he's already here," said Ty. "He arrived early, so I asked Ben to show him around. I think they're down in the barn now."

❧

They walked down the path to find Ben and Jay. As they entered the barn, they heard Ben describing life at Heartland. "All the horses are treated as complete individuals," he was saying. "It's great to see them recover, though to be honest, you wouldn't be involved in the treatment side that much. Amy and Ty do all that. They're fantastic — the most patient people I've ever met."

Amy felt touched at hearing his words but awkward at the same time. Ideally, they *did* want someone who could help with the treatments. Ben had never seemed inclined to do that side of the work.

Ben stopped when he saw them, grinning self-consciously. "Here they are," he finished. "Amy, this is Jay. Jay, Amy. You've already met Ty, right?"

Jay nodded and stepped forward to shake Amy's hand. He was much smaller than either Ben or Ty, with intense dark eyes and loose curls of black hair. Amy wondered how he would fit into an environment like Heartland. The racing world was famous for being tough and ruthless with horses. It seemed unlikely that a stable boy would have the right sort of attitude — but then she pushed the thought away. She would judge him on his own merits.

"I've been showing Jay the stables," said Ben. "I was just about to take him down to see Dazzle, but maybe you'd like to do that."

"Thanks, Ben," said Amy. "Dazzle's paddock is a good place to start."

Leaving Ben to his stable chores, Ty and Amy showed Jay the way to the bottom paddock, chatting with him as they went. Jay was fascinated by everything they did at Heartland and listened intently when they talked about the alternative methods they used.

"Some of those herbs would be great with young race-horses," he commented. "It's difficult to calm them down, though I find massaging them helps."

"You use massage?" Suddenly, Amy was reminded of Ryan, who had been a groom at a leading racing stable. She had met him when Heartland had treated Gallant Prince, a Thoroughbred that had been injured in a fire. Amy had been impressed with the special bond Ryan had shared with Gallant Prince. Ryan was a natural with horses, and Jay had something of the same gentle air about him.

"Yes," said Jay. "I don't know any special method or

anything. I just kind of stroke them. It really chills them out."

They reached Dazzle's paddock. The mustang was grazing at the far end, but he raised his head immediately when Ty whistled.

"He's a beauty," said Jay in admiration. "Is he a mustang?"

"That's right," said Ty. He handed Jay a halter. "Could we watch you catch him? Then we'll take him up to the yard."

Amy wondered if they were giving Jay an unfair task. Dazzle could be so high-strung. Jay entered the paddock with the halter hidden behind his back. The stallion stamped a foreleg and snorted. Jay stood quietly for a minute and didn't stir when Dazzle took a few steps back. Dazzle eyed him again from a safer distance, and Amy could hear Jay murmuring to him in a soft voice. Dazzle flicked his ears, listening. Then Jay turned his back on him and wandered off across the paddock. Dazzle watched him go, looking puzzled. Jay turned to face him once more and carefully stepped toward the stallion. Dazzle allowed him to approach, and without any further fuss, Jay slipped the halter over his head.

Amy smiled as Jay led the mustang to the gate. "That was great," she enthused. "You sure know how to handle horses."

Jay blushed endearingly under his weathered skin. "Well, I work with them every day," he pointed out modestly. "Wouldn't be much use if I hadn't picked up a thing or two by now."

❧

On the front yard, Ty and Amy watched as Jay brushed the mustang down.

"Shall we give him Dazzle to ride?" Ty asked Amy in a low voice. "It'd be interesting to see how he goes for someone else."

Amy nodded. It was a good idea. Dazzle's schooling was almost finished, but he was only used to being ridden by Ty, and sometimes Amy; before he went back to his owners, he would need to behave for more inexperienced riders and riders who didn't know him well.

"Could you tack him up, please, Jay?" Amy called. "I'll go get his tack for you."

Dazzle behaved perfectly as Jay tacked him up. The stable boy had to stand on a bucket to reach the mustang's ears, but Amy was struck by his deft, soothing movements and the way he never did anything to upset or startle the stallion. He was a natural. He hoisted himself easily into the saddle, and Amy and Ty walked alongside him as he rode the mustang down to the training ring.

As Jay deftly maneuvered Dazzle past the gate, Amy

noticed how short his stirrups were, forcing his legs into a tight bend. Ty asked Jay to take Dazzle through some figure eights and serpentines, then over some trotting poles. Before starting, he shortened his stirrups more and took a tight grip on the reins. He then urged Dazzle forward with quick, sharp nudges of his heels. Dazzle was immediately confused and came off the bit, poking his nose in the air and hollowing his back.

Ty grimaced. "I think we should stop him," he said to Amy in a low voice after Jay had circled the ring once. "I don't want to have to completely retrain Dazzle!"

"That's enough, Jay!" called Amy hastily. "Thanks. Can you come back over here?"

Jay rode over looking flustered. "I don't really do this kind of stuff," he said. "But I'm sure I could learn."

Amy smiled encouragingly at him. "That's OK. We'll take Dazzle in now," she said, feeling bad about stopping him so abruptly. "Ty will show you around the rest of the yard and talk you through all the herbs and other remedies that we use."

Jay looked enthusiastic. "OK, that's great," he said, dismounting.

Amy took Dazzle's reins, and the three of them walked back up to the yard. Amy felt really disappointed that Jay's riding wasn't what they were looking for. He had such a gentle touch — perhaps they *could* train him to be more relaxed in his riding style. But realistically, it would take too much time to teach him from scratch. She sighed. Finding someone to replace Ben wasn't going to be as straightforward as she'd imagined.

❧

Over lunch, Amy and Ty discussed Jay's interview while Lou and Grandpa listened.

"He was interested in all the remedies," said Ty regretfully. "He hadn't come across many of them before, but he was so enthusiastic. He'd learn that side of things quickly enough, but his riding . . ." He shook his head.

"Just not up to it," agreed Amy. "We wouldn't be able to let him do any of the exercising, or at least not with horses that need schooling. It's a real shame. He'd be great around the yard."

"Well," said Lou, "that sounds like another rejection to me."

They all looked up as they heard a gentle knock on the door. Lou frowned. "I hope it's not a reporter! We're not expecting another candidate yet, are we?" she said in a hushed voice.

Amy shook her head. "Joni's not due for another half hour or so. Maybe she's early." She went to answer the door. "Sergeant García!" she exclaimed.

"Hello, Amy," said the sergeant. "I thought I'd drop by on my day off. Hope you don't mind."

"No! No, that's fine," said Amy, but her heart was

sinking. "Would you like to come in for a moment, or do you want to see Venture right away?"

Sergeant García hesitated. "I think I'd like to see him, if you don't mind," he said.

"That's fine. I'll just get my coat," said Amy, forcing a smile. How on earth was she going to tell him that they'd made no progress with Venture at all?

Chapter Seven

"I'm afraid we haven't really gotten very far with him yet." Amy opted for the straightforward truth as they approached Venture's stall. "I'm sure we will, but it's going to take time."

Sergeant García didn't look surprised. "I wasn't expecting anything," he said. "I just thought I'd drop in to see him, that's all."

At the sight of his colleague, Venture's ears pricked forward, and he gave a whinny of welcome. The sergeant stepped forward to stroke his neck, and the horse nuzzled him affectionately.

Amy was momentarily filled with hope. "Do you think he seems any better?" she asked.

Mark García shrugged. "Difficult to tell, to be honest," he said. "He's always given me a welcome, even just after the accident." He stepped back and studied Venture more carefully. "He's not the horse he was, I'm afraid. We could walk him out on the yard, if you want me to check for progress."

Amy nodded, but her hope died as quickly as it had surfaced. If Venture's welcome hadn't been anything new, she had a feeling that nothing else had changed, either. She went to grab a lead rope from the tack room and headed back to Venture's stall. Just as she was about to step inside, she stopped.

Mark had cupped one arm under the horse's head and was resting his forehead against Venture's cheek, gently stroking his muzzle with his other hand. His face, usually so calm and controlled, was etched with pain and sadness.

"Poor old boy," she heard him murmur. "When are you going to come back to me? You know I won't go out on the beat without you, friend."

Amy drew in her breath. She swallowed and stepped back for a moment to collect herself. The words were so painfully familiar. *When are you going to come back?* She choked up. Mark's words reminded her of how it had been with Ty — the long days, weeks, that had stretched out with little hope.

She cleared her throat and stepped forward once more. The sergeant looked up, quickly composing himself, and smiled as Amy came back into the stall. Unsure what to say, she slipped the halter over Venture's head and led him out onto the yard.

Venture moved with all his usual reluctance, and after one painful circuit, it was clear that Mark's presence hadn't made any real difference in his movement at all.

Mark watched him, shaking his head. "Poor old Venture," he muttered. "I guess he's reached the end of the road."

Amy was horrified at the resignation in his voice. "Oh, please don't say that!" she exclaimed. "Sergeant García, you shouldn't give up."

The police officer looked at Amy in surprise. "*I* shouldn't give up?" he questioned.

Amy felt momentarily embarrassed. Mark García was so dignified and professional. She could tell he wouldn't be comfortable if he knew that she had seen him just moments before. She hesitated.

"It's just that — well, I kind of understand," she said.

Mark García raised an eyebrow. "You understand?" he echoed.

Amy felt tongue-tied and played with Venture's lead rope.

"Go on," said Sergeant García. "You must mean something by that."

Amy nodded. "Well, yes," she said. "You weren't the only one to have an accident in that storm." She glanced at him quickly, trying to gauge his reaction. His expression was now intense, and Amy could see a little muscle tighten in his jaw. "Our back barn roof collapsed," she went on. Her voice trembled. "There were horses inside. One of them was killed. And Ty was inside, too."

She raised her head. "Ty was in a coma for weeks. Ty and I work together, and nothing seemed the same without him here. I just had to wait, and wait." She paused. "So, you see, I *do* understand."

Sergeant García's face was still. There was a silence, then he reached out and laid his hand on Venture's neck. The big police horse was standing lethargically, resting one hind leg, but he shifted at his rider's touch.

"I . . ." Mark began. His voice cracked, and he stopped to clear his throat. "I didn't know. I'm not sure how that will change things for Venture and me, but thank you for telling me." He stroked Venture's neck for a moment, his face hidden. Then he sighed and turned back to Amy. "Venture came here as a last resort. You knew that, didn't you?"

Amy nodded.

"Sometimes you just have to accept that things are over," he said simply. "After all, no police horse's career lasts forever — no police officer's, either. So when one of the vets suggested sending him here, I didn't allow myself to believe it would make any difference. Nothing else had."

Amy swallowed. "Well, it hasn't yet," she acknowledged humbly. "But I really believe we can reach him, in time."

Mark García nodded but didn't look convinced.

Amy searched his features. All she could see was deep, unhappy resignation. "You will let us keep on trying, won't you?"

Sergeant García stared at his feet. "That's what I'd like," he said eventually. "The problem is, my bosses can't justify the funds it'd take to keep him here indefinitely. But if you think there's a chance . . ." He looked up, his glance questioning.

"Oh, yes," said Amy quickly. "There's always hope. I believe that, I really do. I've had to."

Mark nodded, but his eyes didn't reflect her optimism. "Well, that's something," he said with a little smile. "I'll see what I can do. Maybe we can find a way."

He watched as Amy coaxed the police horse back into his stall, then he leaned on the half door, his chin cupped in his fist. Amy wasn't sure what else to say. The sound of a car pulling up reminded her that the final candidate was due. She let herself out of the stall and caught a glimpse of a blond-haired girl getting out of a taxi.

"I'm afraid I have a meeting now," she said awkwardly. "But please stay with Venture as long as you like."

Sergeant García nodded. "Yes, I'll stick around for a while, if you don't mind."

Amy took a deep breath and went to join Ty, who was already shaking hands with the candidate. Amy reminded herself of her name — Joni Janssen, from Alberta, Canada. Unless she'd been staying locally, she'd come a long way, so Amy realized she must be very interested in the position, if nothing else.

"Hi, I'm Amy," she greeted the girl. "You must be Joni. I hope you're not too tired after your trip!"

"Hi, Amy," said Joni. Her straight blond hair had a chin-length blunt cut so it swung around her face, and her blue eyes had a mischievous twinkle in them. "I'm fine, thank you. I stayed with my uncle in Baltimore last night, so it wasn't too far to come."

Amy warmed to Joni at once. Her accent was subtle, a gentle mix of Canadian and something more lilting. She looked around with interest as they began to show her around the front stable block. When they came to Venture's stall, Amy introduced Sergeant García. Feeling slightly self-conscious, Amy explained why Venture had come to Heartland. She was aware that the sergeant was looking at her and listening gravely.

Joni's face filled with sympathy. "My mom had a horse that was involved in an accident. It took so long for him to get better, but she wouldn't give up on him, and he came around in the end. Mom always says that time's the greatest healer."

Amy noticed that the sergeant had turned to look at Joni. She smiled at him before following Ty to the next stall, and Mark García nodded at her in return.

They moved on to Molly's stall. Curious as ever, the pretty mare had been watching their progress around the yard from over her half door, and she nickered as they approached.

"She's lovely, but she's had a big knock to her confidence recently," Amy explained. "So I'm working on building her trust again, with the help of her owner, Eloise. She's lost some of her confidence, too. That's part of the problem."

Joni reached up and scratched Molly behind the ear. "Do you use Bach Flower Remedies at all? I think I'd give her some larch remedy. It's really good for restoring confidence."

Amy felt pleasantly surprised. "That's exactly what I'm giving her!" she exclaimed.

Joni grinned. "My mom swears by those remedies," she said. "I've only learned some of them so far, though."

"That's great," said Amy. "Do you know about other herbal remedies, too?"

Joni shook her head. "Just the Bach ones. But if there are others that you use here, I'd love to learn about them."

Amy exchanged glances with Ty. He smiled, and she knew that they both had a good feeling about Joni. They asked her to give Molly a quick groom so they could see some of her yard skills. As she did so, she told them a little more about herself. She was seventeen, born in Canada, but her mother was Norwegian and her father Norwegian-American, which meant that she had United States citizenship as well.

"I've finished high school, but Mom wants me to keep on studying," Joni explained, expertly picking up one of Molly's feet. She paused to concentrate while she cleaned out the frog, then put the hoof down again and patted the mare to reassure her. "I'd much rather just start working," she continued. "I don't want to take a big break from being around horses. I wouldn't mind having a place with Mom on the stud farm while taking some practical courses I'm enrolled in, but I wouldn't get to do much riding — and I think she'd pressure me into studying more, anyway. But I figure that if I get a good job really soon, somewhere fantastic like here" — she grinned at Ty and Amy — "she'd let me take it, since I'd still be learning."

She finished with Molly and gave her a rub between her eyes. Ty led the mare back into her stall while Amy took Joni to the tack room.

"We're going to give you Sundance to ride," Amy told her, lifting his saddle from the rack. "Could you take this?"

Joni hoisted the saddle onto her arm, then swung the bridle over her shoulder. Amy led her to Sundance's stall and asked her to tack him up. Amy expected him to be doubly grumpy at being tacked up twice in the same day. She suppressed a smile as Joni led him out of his stall. His whole posture suggested outrage. He dragged his feet and put his ears back, snorting in protest. But Joni took no notice and tacked him up swiftly.

By the time Joni had ridden Sundance down to the training ring, the pony was beginning to realize that she wasn't going to put up with any nonsense. Whenever he started to hunch his back and resist, Joni sat down deep in the saddle and drove him on. Soon he had settled onto the bit and was performing perfect circles in a balanced, rhythmic trot.

"He's a character, isn't he?" Joni commented when Amy called her over to the gate. "He takes a bit to figure out, but I wouldn't have thought he had any real underlying problems."

Amy laughed. "He doesn't," she admitted. "This was kind of a trick question. He's my pony. He can be a bit grumpy, that's all — but you handled him perfectly." She scratched Sundance's neck and gave Joni a warm smile.

℞

By the end of the day, Amy felt exhausted. Meeting people and talking to them was even more tiring than working with the horses! But as she sat down to eat supper, there was little doubt in her own mind that they had found the ideal replacement for Ben.

Nancy had come over to cook supper. It was a feast of roast vegetables and lamb, and Amy eyed the spread hungrily. As everyone ate, she and Ty described all three candidates so that Grandpa and Lou would have a clear idea of what had happened with each. Ben chipped in with his impressions and agreed that Joni stood out from the other two by a long shot.

"It's too bad about Jay," said Amy. "He was so good around the horses. I hope he finds somewhere else soon."

"He will, I'm sure," said Ty. "We can give him some positive feedback. But he definitely needs to improve his riding skills if he's going to work somewhere like Heartland."

Jack nodded. "Yes, it would be good to give him some encouragement, at least," he said. "So it's Joni that you want. But didn't you say something about her living in Canada?"

"That's the only problem," admitted Amy. "She'd have to leave home, and she needs to start work pretty much right away."

She shot a glance at Ben. If Joni started in the near future, it would put pressure on Ben to find a trainer who would take him on as a working pupil — Heartland couldn't afford to let them overlap for long. He might have to leave earlier than he'd planned. But how could they tell him that?

"And she's how old? Seventeen?" asked Grandpa. "I think, in that case, we should help her find somewhere to live. We can't really expect her to figure all that out for herself."

Nancy stood up and started clearing away the plates. "Well," she said, "I would have thought there's an obvious answer to that. She could live here, couldn't she? I'm happy to help out with the cooking and cleaning, so the extra housework wouldn't be a problem. It might be rather nice for you all."

"Live here?" Amy echoed. For a moment, she felt excited. She had liked Joni so much! It would be great to have her living at Heartland. But there was a big problem. "There isn't a spare room," she pointed out.

Nancy looked puzzled. "Yes, there is."

Amy stared at her. There were four bedrooms, only one of which wasn't slept in. And that room had belonged to Marion, her mother. Amy's heart started thudding. Nancy surely wasn't suggesting they use that? She looked across at Grandpa in alarm, hoping that he'd say it wasn't possible. But he had an expression on his face that Amy couldn't read.

Nancy smiled. "And with everything that's happening," she added, looking at Lou, "there'll soon be *two* spare rooms, won't there?"

At this, Lou got to her feet. Her face was like thunder. "How dare you!" she shouted. "First, you interfere with my wedding plans and all the housework and cooking and just about everything else, and now you're telling us how to run Heartland! Where Joni lives is none of your business, and neither is our mother's room. You've no idea what that means to me and Amy, or to Grandpa!"

She stopped, her voice trembling. Amy's mouth dropped open in shock. She looked at Nancy, who had gone deathly pale. Amy saw that her knuckles, clutching the dirty plates, were white.

There was a silence. Everyone looked stunned. Amy was astonished at Lou's outburst. Her sister had seemed a bit annoyed with Nancy at times, but nothing like this! After what seemed like an eternity, Nancy placed the plates carefully on the drain board and turned back to the table.

"Actually, Lou," she said, "I have a very good idea of what that room might mean to you." She walked quickly to pull her coat off the hook, shrugged it on, and picked up her bag.

"I don't think I should come to Heartland for a while," she said quietly, looking at Jack. She opened the door and walked out.

The instant she had gone, Grandpa seemed to pull himself together. He got to his feet and followed her out. Amy heard the sound of Nancy's car starting, then the engine idling for a few minutes before the car headed down the driveway. Everyone sat tensely, waiting for Jack to return. When he appeared in the doorway, he stood still, his face clouded with anger. No one else moved.

"I have no idea why you said what you did, Lou," said Jack. "I simply can't imagine what provoked it. I suppose there must be something, but I'm deeply disappointed in you. In fact, I've never been more disappointed in my life."

Chapter Eight

The mood on the yard was subdued the next morning. Amy had gotten up as usual to work with the horses, but there was no sign of Lou. Amy rode Molly down to the training ring and gave her a basic schooling session, reinforcing the work they had done so far. She wasn't in the mood for trying anything new today.

It had been awkward after Grandpa had come back in. Lou had gone straight to bed, followed shortly by Jack, while Ty and Ben had made their excuses and left. Amy decided to ask Lou out on a trail ride that afternoon. It might cheer her up and give her a chance to talk about things if she wanted to.

Amy rode back up to the yard and tied Molly outside her stall. As she began to untack her, Ben stuck his head over Red's half door.

"Hi, Amy," he called. "Can I talk to you when I'm done with Red?"

"Sure," Amy called back. She wondered what he wanted to talk about. The situation with Joni was tricky. They still hadn't resolved what to do about her accommodations, and Amy didn't want to upset Ben by asking him to leave early. Sometimes she wished Lou would take care of all those aspects of Heartland.

Ten minutes later, Ben reappeared and leaned over Molly's half door.

"I had an idea," he said as Amy brushed Molly's mane. "There's a spare room in the house where I live. I talked to my landlady last night, and she's willing to rent it. Joni could move in there."

Amy stopped brushing. "Really?" Her heart gave a bound of hope, but she looked at Ben doubtfully. "Are you sure?"

"Yes, it should be fine," said Ben. "Then I can drive her to work, no problem. She'll probably get her own car pretty soon, though, won't she?"

"I guess," said Amy. Then she frowned. Ben was talking as though he'd be working alongside Joni, but there wasn't the money to pay two sets of wages.

She hesitated. "Wouldn't you find it a bit much, living and working with the person who's going to take your place?"

"I've thought it all through, Amy," said Ben. "Lou mentioned there's a problem about paying both of us, and I'm happy to let her take over even if I don't have somewhere else to go. Joni's cool. I'm really pleased you've found someone you like. I'll be happy to help her settle in for a few days, then leave. I could still drive her here, though. It's not far."

Amy felt a pang of guilt. Ben was bending over backward to make everything easier for her and for Heartland. But his generosity only made her wonder whether he'd still be leaving if they had made him feel more included in the first place.

"What about Red?" she asked. "You could keep him here, but . . ."

"Don't worry," said Ben. "I'll stable him with my aunt until I find somewhere. I've already asked her if there's room."

"You've thought of everything, haven't you?" said Amy, feeling a strange mixture of sadness and relief. "It's really good of you, Ben. I'll miss you."

"I'll miss you, too," said Ben. He ran a hand through his hair, his expression suddenly miserable. "And everyone else. It might look like I'm getting everything figured out, but, well, at the moment, it doesn't feel like it."

Amy felt a lump rising in her throat. *You don't have to go*, she wanted to say. But she pushed the thought away.

Things had moved way beyond that. "You know you can come back and visit anytime, don't you?" she asked.

Ben nodded. "Thanks." He gave a little smile. "You might eventually regret that."

Amy finished with Molly and went indoors. Grandpa was cooking Sunday brunch as usual, but it seemed odd to see him at the stove by himself. Amy realized she'd grown used to seeing Nancy bustling around the kitchen, joking with him.

She told him about Ben's solution for Joni. "It means she can start as soon as she likes," she said.

"Sounds ideal," agreed Jack, taking some eggs from the fridge. "Well, perhaps we should let her know today."

Amy nodded. "I hope so. I'll speak to Lou about it."

There was still no sign of her sister. Amy went upstairs and knocked on her door. "Lou?" she called softly. "It's me. May I come in?"

She heard a faint yes and opened the door. Lou was sitting on her bed, holding a magazine. But Amy wasn't fooled. She guessed that her sister had shut herself away to think.

"It looks like we've worked out the Joni problem," Amy told her. "She can go and live with Ben — there's a spare room in his boarding house."

Lou ran both hands through her short blond hair, then

let them drop by her side on the bed. "That's good," she said. "Have you called her yet?"

"No. I thought you'd probably need to do it, so you can talk through her contract and everything," said Amy.

"I can deal with all that later. You tell her, if you like."

"OK. Thanks." Amy grinned, then stood in the doorway feeling awkward. "Um — I was wondering if you felt like coming on a trail ride this afternoon. It's a nice day, and a couple of the horses need some exercise."

Lou gave Amy a grateful look. "That sounds good," she said. "Something to blow away the cobwebs."

Amy nodded. "Will you be coming down for brunch?"

Lou smiled. "Yes. I'll see you in a bit." She hesitated, then added, "Thanks, Amy."

Amy ran back downstairs and sifted through the stack of applications to find Joni's cell phone number. She dialed it quickly, feeling excited.

"Hi, Joni," she said when Joni answered the phone. "It's Amy, from Heartland."

"Amy!" said Joni.

Amy could hear a mix of nervousness and anticipation in the girl's voice, and she smiled to herself. It was great to be giving Joni good news. "We'd like to offer you the job, if you're still interested."

"Still interested? Of course I am!" cried Joni. "Oh,

thank you. Thank you. That is the best news ever. I can't believe I got it! How soon can I start?"

"Well, we've managed to work out some of the practical stuff already, so I think you could pretty much start when you like," said Amy, and explained the arrangements that Ben had suggested. "You'll need to discuss the details of your contract with Lou, though."

"That's fantastic," enthused Joni. "I'll just need to run it all by my mom. I'll call you back, is that OK?"

"Fine," said Amy. "I hope she's happy for you to come here. I think you'll fit in really well."

❧

Over brunch, Amy chattered about Joni's arrival, aware that Lou and Grandpa were both much quieter than usual. Ben told everyone about his plans to go back to his Aunt Lisa's yard for a while.

"She should be able to help me find a competition yard," he said. "She's got lots of contacts. She said she'd be interested to see how I've been training Red, too. I think I'm a lot gentler with him than I used to be. We've got a real partnership now."

Amy and Ty exchanged glances. It seemed so long since Ben had arrived. At first, he and Ty hadn't gotten along at all — especially when Ty had seen how harsh Ben could be with his horse. But things had changed as they'd grown to understand each other. Ben had learned to coax the best out of Red by encouraging him and really communicating with him, rather than bullying him. Then, when Ty had first returned to Heartland after being in a coma, Ben had patiently and tirelessly helped him regain his strength. They were now close friends — the kind of friendship that only comes from seeing each other through hardship and change.

The phone rang. Lou went to answer it. When she returned to the table, she had a broad smile on her face.

"Joni is officially a Heartland employee," she announced, sounding much more cheerful than she had earlier. "She arrives on Wednesday."

"Jasmine's obviously glad to be out!" commented Amy that afternoon as she and Lou rode up the track away from Heartland. "She's going really well for you."

"That's good to hear," Lou replied, looking gratified. She pushed Jasmine into a trot and Amy followed on Snowdrop, a recent arrival sent to Heartland for mild reschooling after recovering from an injury. After ten minutes of trotting steadily, Lou looked a lot happier than she did when they left. Amy brought Snowdrop up alongside her, and the sisters rode in silence for a few minutes.

Amy wondered how to get Lou talking about the problems that were hanging in the air. She was still baffled by her sister's outburst. It was one thing for Lou to be moody, but lashing out at Nancy was completely out of character. Amy thought there must have been all sorts of indications that she hadn't picked up on. She felt bad for not being more sensitive. Was this about the wedding? Or just about Nancy?

"So . . . are you still going to let Nancy bake your cake for you?" she asked Lou eventually, not knowing how else to get at the issue.

Lou stiffened. "I don't know yet."

"You do still want to get married, don't you?" asked Amy. It didn't feel like quite the right thing to say, but she was grasping at straws.

"Amy!" Lou exclaimed. "Of course I do."

Her voice shook slightly, and Amy looked across at her in concern.

"Scott's not the problem. I really love him," said Lou in a low voice. She looked down at Jasmine's reins, and Amy suddenly realized that her sister was close to tears. "It's Mom," Lou went on in a strangled voice. "I — I just can't bear the thought of her not being there for the wedding."

Of course. That made perfect sense. It was so obvious that Amy couldn't believe it hadn't occurred to her before. "Oh, Lou," she said softly. "I wish I'd realized."

She brought Snowdrop to a halt and gave him a long

rein so that he could graze. Lou did the same with Jasmine, impatiently brushing a tear from her eye.

"There's no reason why you should," Lou said. "I didn't know I was going to feel this way until it happened. And Nancy — to be honest, I'm not sure why she frustrates me so much. She just does. She keeps sticking her nose in. Nearly every day she comes in, going on about brochures or recipes or dresses or caterers, prompting me for answers — when I don't even *know* what I want yet!"

She paused, fiddling with her reins. "Sometimes," she went on, "when she's nagging me with all these questions, I feel like she can't wait for me to get out so she can take my place."

"Take your place?" Amy asked doubtfully. "What are you talking about? She could never do that!"

But as she spoke, Amy felt a pang of guilt. She had enjoyed having Nancy around. She was a wonderful cook, and it was somehow comforting to have an older woman in the farmhouse. And then it struck her.

"Lou, you know no one could take your place in our family, so maybe it's something else," she said cautiously. Lou slowly raised her head and looked at her sister. She took a deep breath. "Do you think that maybe you are uncomfortable with Nancy because she's doing things that *Mom* would have done?"

Lou looked up at Amy, tears still welling in her blue eyes. "I don't want her taking *anyone's* place!" she burst out, and a large tear of frustration rolled down her face. "Not mine or Mom's or anyone's! I just want everything to stay the same."

Amy felt tears flooding her own eyes. "So do I," she admitted quietly. "I don't want you to go. I'll miss you so much."

"How do you know? Maybe you *won't*," said Lou. "Maybe I'll go and you won't even notice the difference, with Grandpa and Nancy running everything."

Amy shook her head, trying to find the words to say what she knew to be true. "It won't be like that, Lou," she said. "Heartland could never be the same without you. But the thing is, you'll be really happy with Scott. And Mom would have wanted that. She'd have been glad to see you move on. She really would."

Lou took a deep breath and rummaged in her pocket for a tissue. When she didn't find one, she just wiped the sleeve of her barn coat across her nose. "I guess you're right," she said.

Amy sat in silence for some time, letting Lou work through her thoughts. Then she gathered up Snowdrop's reins again and they rode on.

"You know, Nancy's not so bad," Amy said after a while. "Remember how I had trouble accepting Lily and

Helena as part of the family in Australia? You were the one who convinced me to give it some time. Maybe that's what you need to do with Nancy."

Lou gave a small smile. "Maybe."

"I can understand how you feel, though," said Amy. "I couldn't believe it when she suggested giving Mom's room to Joni."

"I know. She's always full of suggestions, but that one was out of line. I couldn't believe she'd be so brazen, and I just snapped." Lou blushed. "I guess I shouldn't have let her get to me. She's really made a big difference to Grandpa."

"He's been a lot happier recently." Amy hesitated. "Maybe Nancy's trying to show interest in us to please him. It must be weird for her if she's never had children of her own."

"Could be. I hadn't thought of it like that," said Lou. She shrugged. "Well, I'll make an effort from now on. Even if it's just for Grandpa's sake. But that doesn't mean I'm going to start sitting down and making cozy wedding plans with her all the time. I have a fiancé for that." Lou gave Amy a quick smile.

"I wouldn't worry. After last night, I don't think she'll be expecting you to," Amy pointed out quietly.

Lou blushed again. She obviously realized she had some apologizing to do, and Amy began to wish she hadn't rubbed it in. She avoided saying anything else by shortening Snowdrop's reins and nudging him forward.

They cantered along the ridge in the crisp winter air, both horses snorting in delight at the chance to stretch their legs. Amy's thoughts returned to what Lou had said about having a wedding without their mom.

"Maybe we could go to Mom's grave sometime soon," Amy suggested when they slowed to a walk again. "We could tell her all about Australia. And if you tell her about getting engaged to Scott, it might make you feel a little better."

Lou nodded. "That would be good." She sighed. "You know, Amy, it's really not that I don't want to get married. I just don't want to rush anything. So much has happened in the last couple of years. I want to be sure that I'm comfortable with where everything is now before I make another big move."

"That makes sense," said Amy. She was glad that she understood Lou's concerns at last — and she couldn't help feeling relieved that her sister wouldn't be disappearing just yet. She could also really relate to Lou's feelings of longing for their mother, so she hoped she would be able to help Lou deal with those emotions. "You know, Lou, Mom would have been so happy about you and Scott," she offered. "She had so much respect for him. I'm sure she would have thought it was the right thing."

Lou smiled. "I'm glad you think so."

"I'm sure of it," Amy said firmly. "I really am."

🙶

It felt so much better to have things out in the open, and Lou and Amy rode back to Heartland in an easy silence. Back on the yard, Amy went to check on Venture, thinking of Sergeant García's visit the day before. She felt strangely honored that she had been given the chance to glimpse past his stoic exterior to the sensitivity that lay just beneath. It would be so wonderful to return Venture to him. Amy knew how much that would mean.

She found Ty in Venture's stall, fiddling with the lightbulb.

"I've changed it to an orange one," he explained to Amy, holding up the old bulb. "It'll be a lot more restful for him."

His voice was flat, and as he pocketed the old bulb and unbolted the stall door, he seemed strangely preoccupied. Amy rested her hand on the half door as Ty walked away, his shoulders hunched. She knew him so well. Instinctively, she ran after him and touched his elbow. "Hey. Are you OK?" she asked.

Ty stopped and shrugged. "Fine," he said.

"Are you sure? It's not — working with Venture, is it?"

Ty gave a little smile and shook his head. "No. It's not Venture."

Amy felt relieved. Ty had been as good as his word with the police horse; he had responded to him just like any other Heartland patient. She searched his face. "There is something, though, isn't there?"

Ty sighed. "Well, OK," he admitted. "The Abrahams called about Dazzle. I explained how far we've come with him, and they decided they'd like to take him home. They're not so concerned about his schooling because they want to use him primarily as a stud horse now."

"Oh, Ty," said Amy. "I'm sorry. You'll miss him so much. When are they coming?"

"This evening," said Ty flatly.

"Today!" Amy exclaimed. "That's so sudden."

"I know. They'll be here in about an hour."

Amy's heart went out to Ty. She touched his arm. "You know, when we went on that trail ride together, I found myself wishing that Dazzle was yours so we could ride together on our own horses all the time." She hesitated. "It doesn't seem fair that you have never had your own horse. I've got Sundance, and I had Storm, too. But you've always had to say good-bye to the horses you work with."

Ty smiled. "I've never wanted that, Amy. I've always been more interested in healing horses and watching them move on to something more. But Dazzle is different. Working with him was a big part of my getting better after the accident. He'll always be special because of that, but I still have to let him go. It's just harder than usual this time."

"I guess," said Amy, a realization slowly dawning on her. "Dazzle reminds you more of the accident than Venture ever could."

Ty drew in a deep breath. "Well, not so much the accident itself," he said slowly. "To be honest, I don't remember much of what happened that night. But Dazzle's been an important part of my recovery. Every day I struggled to make it here, I knew he'd be in the paddock. He gave me a short-term goal." His green eyes looked intensely into Amy's. "But you know, Amy, I wasn't the one who was brave when we took on Venture. I wasn't the one who had to witness everything and then just wait to find out if things would ever improve."

Amy flushed slightly. "I think Soraya saw it that way, too," she admitted. "But it's not like that. I'm getting a chance to make things better, to try to give Sergeant García back part of his life that was taken away."

"But you know how he feels," said Ty.

Amy nodded and raised her eyes to Ty's, a wave of emotion rising through her. She took a deep breath. "I'll make sure I'm around when the Abrahams come for Dazzle."

"Thanks," said Ty. He smiled. "It's good to know that

neither of us has to go through those things on our own anymore."

℞

Dazzle pricked his ears, his nostrils flaring, when the Abrahams pulled into the yard with their trailer.

"You've done an amazing job with him!" exclaimed Mrs. Abrahams when Ty led him forward. "He's such a beauty. We can't wait to see what his first foals will be like."

"I'm sure they'll be gorgeous," said Amy.

"What would you say if we sent one of them to you for training?" asked Mr. Abrahams. "Now that we've seen evidence of your work, I don't think we'd trust anyone else. I would never have guessed that Dazzle could be so easy to handle."

Amy thought of Daybreak and Solly, two of the young horses she had helped train. They had both gone back to their owners before she'd had a chance to take them through all the stages of schooling. It would be so exciting to train a foal from the beginning. "That would be fantastic," she said. "Please do."

She watched as Ty guided Dazzle up the ramp. Dazzle was understandably nervous — after all, the last time he had seen the inside of a trailer was when he was still terrified of human contact. But his trust in Ty was absolute. With a little gentle coaxing, the stallion stepped up into the dark interior.

Amy felt a lump grow in her throat as she saw Ty give the stallion a final hug and tousle of the mane. He murmured something in his ear. Then Ty stepped back down the ramp, and Amy held out her hand. Ty squeezed it as Mr. Abrahams lifted the ramp and bolted the trailer door.

"Nothing ever stays the same, does it?" Amy whispered to him as the Abrahams gave a final wave and climbed into the cab.

"No," Ty whispered back. "But, you know, I really think that's OK."

Chapter Nine

"Amy! Joni's here!" Lou shouted up the stairs.

"I'm coming!" called Amy, pulling on her jeans.

It was Wednesday evening, and Joni had arranged to come straight to Heartland for dinner before going to see her new lodgings with Ben.

Amy bounded down the stairs and headed outside, where she found Ty and Ben showing Joni around the yard again. She had stopped at Molly's stall and was giving her a lot of fuss, which she was clearly enjoying.

"Hi, Joni," Amy greeted her. "Good to see you!"

"Hi!" said Joni. "I'm just meeting all the horses again. It's going to be great, getting to know them. I think I'm good friends with Molly already."

"Can we drag you away from her for some dinner?" asked Amy, laughing.

Joni grinned. She gave Molly a final pat on the neck and straightened the mare's forelock. Then everyone piled inside to eat.

Jack was helping Lou serve. The atmosphere between them had improved over the last few days, and Amy guessed that Lou had apologized to him, at least. But Nancy still hadn't been back.

"You'll have to tell me about all the horses and what you're doing with them," said Joni, enthusiastically cutting into Lou's cheese-and-potato pie. "Then I'll see how much I can remember in the morning!"

Amy and Ty took turns explaining which horses were Heartland residents and which had come for treatment. Ben chipped in every now and again, explaining where he had been able to help out.

Joni listened avidly. "I can't wait to start," she declared. "What time do you get here in the morning, Ben?"

"You don't need to worry about getting here early tomorrow," said Jack. "You'll need time to settle in to your new place."

"Oh, I don't care about that," said Joni cheerfully. "I'd much rather come with Ben and get started."

Amy smiled across the table at her. Joni seemed to feel at home already — and Amy had the feeling they were going to get along famously.

❧

The next morning, Joni was as good as her word, ready bright and early to start work. When Amy started her daily session with Molly, the new stable girl came to watch, curious to know how the mare was progressing.

"She's been doing really well through muddy patches, small piles of straw, stuff like that," explained Amy, leading Molly out of her stall. "She's so much more trusting than she was. But she's still got to deal with her fear of putting her feet in water. That's the thing she's most anxious about, because it's how she got injured."

Joni nodded. "How are you going to tackle it?"

"I'm going to set the hose going so that it makes a really shallow stream. There's a slight dip in the yard on the way to the far paddock, so it'd be perfect," said Amy. "I'll lead her through it first, and if she's OK with that, we can move on to riding her through it."

"Sounds good," said Joni. "I can do the prep work with the hose, if you like."

Molly's trust in Amy had continued to grow, and she only spooked a little as they approached the water. Amy allowed the mare to take her time. She bent down to sniff it, nosing it with her soft muzzle. Amy thought Molly might fidget a bit, eyeing the glistening stream from different angles, but instead she instantly responded to Amy's gentle tug on her halter and walked straight through it.

"Bravo!" called Joni, turning off the water at the tap. "That was great."

Amy smiled. "I'll try tacking her up and riding her through it now," she said.

Joni held Molly while Amy got her tack, then helped her fasten the buckles on the mare's bridle and reach for the girth underneath her belly.

"D'you need a leg up?"

"No, I'll be fine, thanks," responded Amy, swinging herself lightly into the saddle. "Come on, Molly. Let's see how brave you'll be for me."

If anything, having Amy on her back seemed to offer Molly more reassurance. Amy nudged her forward with a gentle squeeze of her calves, and she stepped through the water without hesitation.

"You know what else you could do?" said Joni. "You could try running water over her legs with the hose. She's probably had that done before, after muddy rides or hard workouts — but it'll all help her get used to being in water again."

"Great idea," said Amy.

She dismounted, and Joni turned the hose on Molly's feet. As she did so, it slipped, spraying Amy with water.

"Hey!" yelled Amy, laughing. "It's not *my* feet that need hosing."

"Sorry, Amy," giggled Joni. "Didn't mean it. Honest." Molly flickered her ears at the sound of the girls laughing and seemed unperturbed by the water shooting over her hooves. Joni hosed her hind legs, too, just for good measure.

"A good morning's work," said Amy as they led Molly back to her stall. "I just wish I didn't have to go to school. I'll have to hand you over to Ben and Ty now."

Later that evening, when Ben had taken Joni home, Amy and Ty sat in the tack room discussing how her first full day had gone.

"Absolutely no problems," Ty said. "Joni's great. She really pitched in with all the yard work. At one point there was nothing much for her to do, so she just sat and cleaned a whole load of tack without being asked."

"That's great," said Amy, looking around at the racks of saddles, the leather worn yet conditioned. "It's a shame that Ben has to go."

"Yes," agreed Ty. "He's arranged with his aunt to take Red away on Saturday afternoon. That'll be his last workday, too."

The finality of it suddenly hit Amy again.

She lapsed into silence, resting her head on Ty's shoulder. She couldn't help but think of how much Ben had done for Heartland, especially in the last months when things had been the hardest. There had been so much thankless work to do, and it had always gotten done. And now, just as things were supposed to be back to normal, he was leaving. "It's just all happened so quickly," she said. "We're not even going to have time to give him a proper send-off. It's too late to organize something for tomorrow night. I heard him say he's going out."

"I don't think he expects anything," said Ty. "But I guess it would have been nice."

"Maybe we can do something for him later," Amy thought out loud. "I'll talk to Lou. We can't just let him *go* like that."

"No," agreed Ty. He kissed the top of her head. "It's nice of you to have thought of it. Ben's lucky to have you for a friend."

Amy smiled up at him and shook her head. "I think I'm the one who's been lucky," she said.

🙞

Red seemed to know it was a momentous occasion as Ben led him toward the trailer. He looked magnificent in his traveling rug, every inch a future champion, with his ears pricked forward and his nostrils flaring. He clattered up the ramp without any fuss.

"Do you have everything?" asked Amy. "I've taken a quick look around the tack room, but I didn't see anything else of Red's."

Ben grinned. "I don't think I need to worry, anyway," he said. "Something tells me I'll be back soon enough."

"You'd better," said Amy. She knew that she'd feel upset when the time came, but she still couldn't hold back the tears. She stepped forward to give Ben a hug, remembering everything they had been through together. She still wondered if there was some way that she could have convinced him to stay.

"Thanks for everything," whispered Ben, and she thought she heard a catch in his voice. She drew back, unable to speak.

Ben shook hands with Jack and hugged Ty and Lou. Then they all gathered around as he climbed into the driver's seat. He started the engine, and the trailer roared to life.

"Take care!" called Ben, with a wave.

"Bye, Ben!" everyone chorused. "Good luck! See you soon!"

When the trailer had turned onto the road and disappeared, Amy looked around for Joni. She had kept a respectful distance while everyone had been seeing Ben off, and Amy found her grooming Sugarfoot in the back barn.

"Good-byes are awful, aren't they?" said Joni sympathetically. "I had a hard time saying good-bye to my mom and dad. Mom was really upset."

Amy nodded silently, not trusting herself to speak on

the subject. Joni handed her the hoof pick, and Amy felt grateful to her for understanding that she didn't want to talk about it. She bent down to pick the little pony's feet, hiding her face until she'd recovered.

"I was wondering how things are going with Venture," said Joni after a while. "Ty was telling me a bit about him yesterday."

Amy put down the last hoof and straightened up, beginning to feel a bit better. "Not as well as I'd like, actually. Do you want to go to his stall and look at him?" she suggested. "We're treating him with all the herbs and flower remedies we can, but they're not having much effect."

As they walked back up to the front yard, Amy explained more about the trauma that Venture had suffered and how it was difficult to pinpoint the source of the pain.

"He's so depressed," she said. "And there have been no fluctuations. The pain is constant, and nothing seems to bring him any comfort. We can't do join up because he's unwilling to move around. And we keep getting phone calls from journalists asking how he is, which makes it seem worse."

They reached Venture's stall and slipped inside. Amy told Joni which remedies they were using — Star of Bethlehem and Rock Rose Flower Remedies, and lavender oil for massages. Joni listened intently, then ran her fingers lightly over the horse, gauging his reaction to pressure in different places.

"I wish my mom could see him," she said. "I'll ask her about him next time I talk to her. She's fantastic with horses like this."

"She's a vet, right?" asked Amy curiously.

"Yeah. But she's qualified in all sorts of other things, too. And she's really into the Bach Remedies, like I told you."

"Sounds a lot like my mom," said Amy with a little smile.

Joni looked at her questioningly but didn't say anything. Amy was glad. She didn't feel like explaining her whole history right then. There was just too much going through her head, and it was good to see that Joni knew where to draw the line.

"Do you think we could go to the cemetery tomorrow, Lou?" Amy asked later. "I'd really like to go soon."

The two sisters were washing the dishes after dinner. Lou put a stack of plates into the cupboard and nodded. "That should be OK. I'm planning to see Scott after brunch for a couple of hours, but we could go after that."

"I'd like to get some flowers," said Amy. "I guess that means a detour."

"No problem," said Lou. "That's a good idea."

After explaining to Ty where they were going, Lou and Amy drove off the next day in the midafternoon. The weather was mild, and Amy felt for the first time that spring was in the air. She bought a hand-tied bunch of spring flowers to put on Marion's grave, and Lou chose some delicate yellow roses.

As they neared the cemetery, they both became quiet, lost in their own thoughts. They left the car and made their way to the familiar gravestone on the opposite side of a gentle slope, nestled close to a cluster of maple trees.

"Do you want to go first?" asked Amy.

"OK. Thanks," said Lou, stepping forward to prop her flowers against the cold stone.

Amy wandered off while Lou stood alone at Marion's grave. They had developed a system, so they both had a chance to talk to their mother on their own. Amy could hear the soft murmur of her sister's voice, but not what she said. She waited for a while, casting sidelong glances to check when Lou had finished. Lou gave her a quick, tremulous smile as she walked away. Then Amy stepped forward and placed her bunch of flowers next to Lou's.

"Hi, Mom," she said softly, kneeling down as she spoke. "I've got so much to tell you. Ben's just left, and even though he never knew you, it's made me miss you more than ever. I tried to make him stay, but I guess he needs to move on. So now we have a new stable hand named Joni. She talks about her mom a lot."

Amy paused as her tears began to fall. Then she brushed them away with her sleeve and went on. "I think you'd like her, Mom. She's great with the horses and already knows a lot of the remedies we use. She's a lot of fun, too. But it was really sad to see Ben go. He's decided to concentrate on competing. I guess he's like you and Dad were when you were young."

Amy stopped to think about how her father's show-jumping accident had ended his competitive career. It was only after that accident that her mom had decided to start Heartland — until then, Marion had belonged to the world of competitions, too.

"I keep learning, Mom," Amy continued. "Ben leaving has taught me to accept that not only horses move on from Heartland. People have to go, too. I wish these lessons weren't so hard. Sometimes, I just wish you were here."

She stayed at the graveside until Lou joined her. Amy stood up, and they silently clasped hands. Then, as if knowing instinctively when the other was ready to go, they both turned to leave.

It was nearing dusk as they made their way back toward the car, each lost in her own thoughts. In the dimming light, a movement caught Amy's eye.

"Lou! Look," she said in a low voice, pointing across

to the other side of the graveyard. There was a figure standing alone in front of one of the graves.

"Is that Nancy?" murmured Lou, pulling Amy to a stop. "I wonder what she's doing here?"

The older woman hadn't seen them. She stood for some time with her head bowed, then turned and walked slowly back to her car. Amy and Lou watched her get in and drive away.

"Her husband must be buried here," said Amy. Jack had told them that Nancy had been widowed several years before.

Lou nodded. "Shall we go look at the gravestone?"

The two sisters followed the gravel paths around to the spot where Nancy had been standing. Amy felt a little nosy, creeping around a cemetery to read about other people's relatives. It felt like she was trespassing. A fresh bouquet of scarlet tulips lay next to a pristine marble headstone.

"'My dearly beloved husband, Edward Marshall,'" Lou read aloud. "She's been a widow for almost ten years."

Amy stepped back, not wanting to intrude anymore. As she did so, she noticed that there was an identical bouquet of tulips on the next grave down. She glanced at the headstone and her mouth went dry.

"Lou," she whispered.

"What is it?"

Amy pointed, unable to speak. They read the headstone in silence.

IN LOVING MEMORY OF JENNIFER MARSHALL, BORN NOVEMBER 2, 1968, DIED FEBRUARY 27, 1983. OUR DEAREST JEN, TAKEN TOO SOON.

Lou and Amy stared at each other.

"Do you think . . . ?" Amy began.

Lou's eyes filled with tears. "She had a daughter," she said, her voice breaking. "Nancy must have had a daughter."

Chapter Ten

❧

Lou and Amy drove back to Heartland in shock. They found Jack in the living room reading the newspaper, and they sat down on the sofa next to him.

"Grandpa," Lou began slowly. "Did you know that Nancy had a daughter?"

Jack looked up sharply. "Pardon?"

"Amy and I were just at the cemetery," Lou explained. "We saw Nancy there. She'd left flowers on the grave of someone named Jennifer Marshall, who died when she was fourteen."

Now it was Grandpa's turn to look shocked. Amy suddenly realized what it might mean to him, and her heart beat faster. He, too, had lost his daughter. Why wouldn't Nancy have told him? After all, she knew about Marion.

"Maybe it wasn't her daughter," Amy said uncertainly, wishing what she said might be true.

"It had to be," Lou insisted. "Why else would she be buried next to Nancy's husband?"

Grandpa still looked stunned. "I've seen pictures in her house," he said at last, "of a fair-haired girl. She looks a bit like Nancy, but I always assumed it was her niece. . . ."

"I guess it explains a lot," said Amy, thinking of the night that Nancy had left. *I have a very good idea of what that room might mean to you*, she'd said. It all made sense now, knowing that she had also struggled with loss.

Grandpa nodded, looking at Lou. "Well . . ." he began.

Lou's gaze dropped to the floor.

"I guess we should go and visit Nancy," Amy said quietly.

"Yes," whispered Lou. "I need to apologize. She needs to know that we understand."

"Hey, Amy!" Joni called cheerily as Amy trudged toward the paddock in her school clothes. "Good day at school?"

Amy made a face. "The usual. I'll just go and change. I'll be back in a minute."

Amy threw on her barn clothes. She was relieved to

be home. She hated being at school when she could be helping Joni settle in, but at least she was back now. She hurried down to the front stable and found Joni leaning over Venture's door.

"Any improvement?" asked Amy, coming up behind her.

Joni shook her head. "I've got an idea, though," she said. She hesitated. "I don't want to interfere or anything, but I've been talking to my mom, and she asked if you'd thought of trying acupuncture."

"Acupuncture?" Amy asked, her eyebrows rising. "I don't know much about it, to be honest."

"My mom's a practitioner," Joni went on. "It's one of the things she trained in after she became a vet. We use it a lot on our brood mares. It's great for dealing with physical pain, but it's also a holistic treatment. You can use it to get to the bottom of emotional pain, too."

Hearing that description, Amy was interested, but she was still uncertain of the procedure. "Doesn't it require piercing the skin with needles? Venture can't even handle T-touch."

"That's the amazing thing — it doesn't really hurt, not like getting a shot. It's based on Chinese medicine," Joni explained. "It's all about the body having a constant flow of energy along lines called meridians. When you're unhealthy or injured, the channels can get blocked or unbalanced, so the energy doesn't flow right. Acupuncture works on unblocking the meridians with really fine needles so that the energy can flow freely again and the body can heal itself."

"But how do you know which channels are blocked?" Amy asked, thinking about how Venture seemed stiff and achy everywhere.

"By assessing all the symptoms, basically," said Joni. "But it's more complex than that. You have to know all about anatomy. The channels have places called points, which is where you put the needles in."

"And it really works?" Amy was fascinated.

Joni shrugged and laughed. "It seems to. Scientists can't explain why, but it's been practiced for thousands of years. My mom swears by it. I'm learning all the principles myself so that I can practice acupressure, which is like acupuncture without the needles. You can do that without being a vet."

Amy's curiosity was piqued. Venture's treatment had been going so badly that it was good to hear about something — anything — that might help. "Do you really think it's the answer for Venture?"

Joni nodded. "It can work when conventional methods aren't effective. I need to talk to my mom again, but she's coming down in a few days with a load of my stuff, so if she thinks it's the right thing, she could treat Venture herself."

"That's great news!" exclaimed Amy. "We have to tell Ty — let's go find him!"

They ran down to the training ring where Ty was lunging a new arrival, Indigo. He reined the horse in when he saw them approaching the gate and walked over. He listened intently to what Joni had to say, then nodded.

"I've heard of acupuncture being good for horses," he said. "The problem is that we don't know anyone who is qualified to do it."

"That's the best part," enthused Amy. "Joni's mom is coming down soon. She'll be able to treat Venture herself."

"Sounds great," said Ty. Then he frowned. "We need to make sure that Scott's fine with it first. And Sergeant García. They have to give their OK."

Joni looked slightly anxious. "My mom's a qualified vet," she said. "She works with lots of horses back home."

"Sure," said Ty gently. "But Scott is Venture's vet while he's at Heartland. We have to run something like this by him."

Amy knew that Ty was right, but she felt sorry that their enthusiasm had been dampened all the same. "I don't mind calling Scott," she offered, giving Joni a warm smile. "I'll call him after supper. And Sergeant García, too."

❧

To her surprise, Amy felt slightly nervous when it came to making the phone calls. She didn't know anything about acupuncture herself, and Joni was so new . . . it could be awkward if the procedure wasn't a success — especially if the press found out and made a big deal of it.

She decided to phone Mark García first. He sounded surprised to hear from her, but there was a warmth in his voice that she hadn't registered before. She explained that they wanted to try a new kind of treatment.

"Obviously, we can't be sure if it will be effective," she explained. "And we'd need your permission before we go ahead."

"It sounds like a good idea to me," said Mark. "I'm willing to try anything, and I appreciate your trying so many methods. I have a lot of respect for your tenacity. It's a fine quality, you know."

"Thanks!" Amy felt touched, and slightly embarrassed. "Well, that's what we do at Heartland."

"Yes. I've been thinking about what you told me," the police sergeant said. "And I think you're right. I need to keep holding on to the hope that he'll recover. That's what's important now."

"That's good to hear. And everyone else is OK with

that?" asked Amy anxiously. "Everyone at the police department, I mean?"

Mark García gave a sigh. "Well, it's been quite a week," he admitted. "There are obviously all sorts of prioritization issues in our department when it comes to funding. They've already put so much into vet bills. But I've made my case. My bosses have agreed to continue Venture's treatment — as long as I partly fund it myself."

Amy drew in her breath.

"So I've agreed to it. I have savings," he went on. "It's the least I can do." He paused. "I might easily have given up. But you helped me see beyond that. I'm with you — and Venture — whatever it takes."

"I'm so pleased," Amy said warmly. "I know it's the right decision. I really do."

She hung up the phone, her optimism surging. As long as Scott agreed as well, they might really be getting somewhere. Amy dialed Scott's number with her heart thumping.

"Acupuncture?" mused Scott on the other end of the line. "Well . . ." he hesitated. "There's no guarantee it'll work, you know. As far as I'm aware, it's not widely used on horses yet."

"But do you think it might be worth trying?" Amy persisted. "I mean, would you allow us to try it on Venture? Joni's mom's a vet and she uses it all the time on their horses."

"I wouldn't say no," said Scott cautiously. "If it's carried out properly it couldn't do any harm. I'd just be careful about getting your hopes up too high, that's all."

Amy breathed a sigh of relief. They could go ahead, at least. "Thanks, Scott. I understand what you're saying. We won't expect miracles. I'm just glad there's something else we can try. It might be Venture's last hope."

❧

With all the excitement about Venture, it was difficult to concentrate at school the next day. Moreover, Amy had agreed with Lou that they would visit Nancy right after school. She was anxious at the prospect, and Amy knew she'd be glad when it was over — but not half as glad as Lou would be.

"I hope she's home," said Lou as they drove through town later that day. "I don't know if I'd have the courage to do this twice!"

"I know what you mean," said Amy.

"I just feel so bad," Lou went on. "I never should have said that to her. It was so selfish of me."

Amy gave her sister a sympathetic smile. She was glad she could be there for moral support. It wasn't often that Lou needed it, but the disagreement was still hanging over the whole family. Amy knew that Grandpa had visited Nancy a few times since that night, but there had been no mention of when she might come back to Heartland. Amy suspected that was because it was up to Lou to make amends.

Nancy's house was painted a pale eggshell blue, the small front garden densely planted with rose bushes that were still bare since winter had yet to wane. Lou and Amy made their way up the path to the front door. Lou took a deep breath and rang the bell.

The house was very quiet, and it seemed forever before they heard the sound of footsteps in the hallway. The door opened and Nancy stood there, holding gardening gloves in one hand. She stared at them for a moment, then quickly recovered and smiled.

"Why, this is a nice surprise!" she said. "Will you come in? I can make us some tea."

Amy and Lou followed her through the house to the kitchen, which had a back door leading onto a porch overlooking the back garden.

"It's such a lovely day, I've been outside, getting it ready for some spring planting. It won't be long now," said Nancy, keeping her smile bright as she filled the kettle and switched it on. She bustled around, bringing out a tray and a set of china teacups. She placed them on a wooden table. "Would you like to sit down? I love this view. I have my breakfast here every morning."

Amy gently pulled out a chair, all the while looking

out through large windows into the garden. Gardening was obviously one of Nancy's great loves; even though the spring flowers had not yet started making an appearance, Amy could picture what the garden was like in full color.

She and Lou were just sitting down when Nancy came back.

"What kind of tea would you like? My favorite is Earl Grey. It was Edward's favorite, too, you see. But I know it's not to everyone's taste — I haven't converted Jack yet. He's so devoted to his coffee!" She gave a little laugh.

"Do you have any peppermint tea?" Lou asked.

"Yes, I think so," said Nancy. "How about you, Amy?"

"I'll try the Earl Grey," said Amy. "Thanks."

Nancy disappeared again, leaving them to stare out into the garden. Lou was restless and stood up again to wander to the window. Amy joined her and they looked out over the well-kept lawn — very different from the tiny garden at Heartland, which had been rather neglected since Marion died.

"It's a beautiful garden," Amy commented when Nancy returned. "You must put a lot of work into it."

Nancy placed the tea tray on the coffee table. "Well, it keeps me busy," she said. "Keeps my mind off things." She handed a cup to Lou. "Here's your peppermint tea.

I've made a pot for us, Amy. It's a shame I didn't know you were coming. I could have made some cookies."

They watched as Nancy laid out cups and saucers and poured the tea.

Lou took a deep breath. "I'm sorry we didn't call ahead, but I guess you know why we've come," she began. "I . . . I'd like to say I'm sorry."

Nancy passed a cup over to Amy and settled back into her chair. "Yes. I thought that might be it," she said quietly.

Lou took a sip of her tea, then placed it back in the saucer. "There's no excuse really . . . for what I said. . . ." She stopped. "I didn't expect to find it so hard, having someone else around at Heartland. Someone . . . older. I overreacted, to say the least."

"I understand," said Nancy. "No one can replace your mother." She looked down at the teacup in her hands. "It hasn't been easy for me either, spending time with a family again. It's brought back a lot of memories."

To Amy's dismay, Nancy's eyes filled with tears. Amy wanted to reach out to Nancy — to let her know that they understood.

"We saw you in the graveyard on Sunday," Amy said softly. "We were there putting flowers on Mom's grave."

"And we guessed that Jennifer was your daughter," Lou put in.

Nancy nodded. The tears in her eyes spilled over, and

she quickly pulled a handkerchief from her sleeve to dab them.

"I'm so sorry," said Lou. "I didn't know. None of us did."

"No. I know. It was silly of me," said Nancy, her voice trembling. "I just thought that you all had enough grief of your own, without knowing about mine. I was wrong. It happened so long ago, but the pain can still feel new."

Amy felt her sadness for Marion welling up all over again. Would it ever begin to fade? Nancy was still grieving for her daughter many years after her death. Perhaps the pain never went away. Amy took a gulp of her tea and realized that her hands were shaking.

There was silence for a moment.

Lou put her teacup back on the table. "I know what you mean. Somehow it makes new experiences hard — even happy ones . . . like a wedding. . . ." She trailed off.

"Oh yes, it must be difficult thinking of that day without your mother," Nancy offered in a sympathetic tone. "I know I'd always imagined Jennifer's wedding day."

Amy saw the anguish in her eyes and understood. Just as Lou longed for Marion to be able to share her wedding, Nancy must have hoped to see Jennifer married, with a long happy life in front of her.

Nancy blew her nose. "I'm so glad you both came. At least everything's out in the open now. It can't change what we've all been through, but talking helps ease the pain a little."

Lou nodded. "Thank you for being so understanding. I'm still sorry, but I'm glad it gave us a chance to talk. I'm really glad we came." She stood up. "We ought to get back. Grandpa's cooking supper for us, and he'll give us a hard time if we're late. Can we help you clear away the dishes?"

"No, no, you get going," said Nancy. "I know how busy you both are."

She ushered them to the door, back to her usual bustling self.

"Thanks so much for everything, Nancy." Lou leaned forward to give the older woman a kiss on the cheek.

Amy stepped outside, then turned impulsively and gave Nancy a hug. "Come back to Heartland soon," she said. "I've missed you."

Nancy looked surprised and pleased. "Why, thank you, Amy," she said. "I'm sure I'll drop by before long." She turned to Lou, a mischievous look in her eyes. "And don't forget. I'm still happy to bake that cake — if you'll let me!"

Chapter Eleven

"That's it, show her you're feeling confident. Give nice, firm commands," called Amy, as Eloise nudged Molly forward through a mound of dead leaves that Amy had arranged in the training ring. "Don't give her a chance to feel you're doubting her."

Eloise sat deep in the saddle and drove Molly on, and to the rider's obvious delight, the mare dropped her nose onto the bit and walked confidently through the leaves. Amy saw the excitement on Eloise's face and grinned. "This is the best part," she said to Joni, who was sitting on the fence beside her. "Seeing a horse change, and knowing she's almost ready to go back to her owner."

Joni nodded. "I believe that," she said. "They look so good together."

Amy left Joni at the gate and jogged over to Eloise and Molly in the center of the training ring. "Now for the big test," Amy said to Eloise. "I want you to ride her through water. We've given her lots of preparation so she should be fine. The key is going to be your confidence, not hers. Do you think you're ready for that?"

Eloise looked nervous, then smiled. "You've done a fantastic job with her, Amy," she said. "Do you really think she'll be OK?"

"Yes, I do," said Amy. "She's been fine going through water for about a week now. If she doesn't have problems doing it with me, there's no reason why she'd be different with you."

She led the way out of the training ring and up onto the track that led to Clairdale Ridge. Joni joined her and they walked alongside Molly, chatting with Eloise.

"There's a little stream that runs across the path up here," Amy explained. "You can try riding her through that. Just remember — all you have to do is believe in her. Then she'll have confidence in you."

"OK," said Eloise. "You know, she's going so well, I *do* believe in her."

Amy looked at the mare, who was walking along with her ears pricked and her neck arched. Curious as ever, Molly was clearly delighted to be out on the trails, but she wasn't pulling or fidgeting. She was listening to her rider and responding willingly to her commands.

"There you go," said Amy, stopping and pointing along the track. "The stream's just ahead. It cuts straight through the path. We'll stay here and watch so we don't get in the way."

Eloise took a deep breath and nudged Molly on. The horse continued up the dirt path, then stopped when she spotted the stream. It wasn't particularly deep, but it was fast-flowing, gurgling over pebbles and glinting in the light that filtered through the trees.

"Come on, Molly," said Eloise firmly. "We're going through it."

She gave her a determined squeeze with her calves, and Molly stepped forward tentatively, placing one hoof in the stream. Amy saw the mare stiffen as her foot disappeared into the water. But Eloise kept up the pressure. Molly took another step, then another, until she had walked right through it. On the other side, Eloise turned in the saddle and gave a whoop of triumph.

"We did it!" she called back. "I can't believe it!"

Amy and Joni laughed. "Bring her back then!" Amy called.

This time, Molly didn't even hesitate. She splashed through the stream, her hooves covered to the fetlocks. Eloise broke into a trot to rejoin the others. Happily, they set off back down the track to Heartland.

"It feels so good to have her trust again. Do you think

I can take her home soon?" Eloise asked as they entered the yard.

Amy nodded. "As soon as you like," she said with a smile.

❧

Lou was humming a tune when Amy went inside for supper. Her whole mood seemed to have lifted since their visit to Nancy a couple of days earlier. Grandpa was clearly just as pleased, and to Amy's relief, the family atmosphere was very much back to normal.

"Eloise is coming to pick up Molly on Sunday," Amy told her. "We have quite a few spaces now — Dazzle and Red have gone, Molly's stall will be free . . ."

"OK, I'll have a look at the waiting list," said Lou. "I'll take care of it."

"There's something else," said Amy. "I feel really bad that we didn't give Ben a farewell party. Do you think we could do something for him soon?"

Lou looked dismayed. "Amy, you're right! Why didn't you mention it before? Of course. When were you thinking of?"

"Well, it might be better to wait until Joni's mom leaves," said Amy. "She gets here tomorrow for the first of Venture's acupuncture treatments. It'd probably be best to have it on a weekend. Maybe next Saturday?"

Lou grabbed her calendar and checked the dates. "That should be fine," she said. "Do you want to check with him if that's OK?"

Amy nodded. "I'll ask when he brings Joni over tomorrow," she replied.

℞

The next morning, Amy made sure she was in the yard when Ben and Joni arrived. She waved to Ben to stop him from driving off right away. Amy thought that was odd to see his truck pull into the drive and then back up and turn around to leave so quickly — it still was though he should be getting out to join in with the chores.

"Ben! Can I talk to you?" she called.

Ben hesitated and then shut off the engine before getting out of his truck. "Sure."

"We were wondering if you'd come over to dinner one night," said Amy. "We never got to give you a proper going-away party. I hope it isn't too late to let you know how much you'll be missed."

"That'd be great," said Ben. "I wasn't expecting anything . . . but you know, I miss you guys already." He looked around the yard and let his gaze rest on Joni, who was just visible, already mucking out the stalls.

Amy smiled. "Yeah. I know. It's not the same without you around."

Ben gave a little shrug. His eyes were still on Joni's back, bent over her fork. "It's nice of you to say so, Amy," he said. "But I can see that Joni really fits in, more than I ever did. I guess, in a way, she was what you needed all the time."

Amy's eyes flew wide open. "Ben! That's not how it was at all. You were amazing. You did so much. I don't know what we would have done without you, especially when . . . when everything went wrong. In fact I don't blame you for deciding to leave." She found herself saying exactly what she'd been thinking ever since Ben resigned. "We put so much on you at the end. There was so much to do that you never really got a chance to treat the horses, or even really work with Red."

"No, no, no," Ben interrupted her. "Don't think that. Please." He shook his head vehemently, then ran a hand through his hair. "You and Ty did everything you could to get me involved," he said. "It was my decision. I learned a lot, but I could never take my attention away from Red for long enough to really delve into it."

"Do you really believe that?" Amy asked slowly. "Because I feel bad. I wish I'd done more."

"You did more than you know," Ben reassured her. "And that means a lot."

They looked at each other, and Amy thought of what Ty had said. *Ben's heart doesn't belong here.* Still, it was good to hear him say so himself, even though it was difficult to understand. But now, seeing him leaning on the door of his pickup, she was beginning to accept it at last.

"We were thinking of next Saturday for the party," she said, finally feeling like there was something to celebrate. "Will that be OK?"

Ben bit his lip. "Could be tricky. I'm competing that day," he said. He thought for a minute, then his face cleared. "It's an afternoon class, so maybe you and Joni could watch me jump? Then we can all come back here together afterward."

Amy nodded enthusiastically. "Well, of course we don't want *your* party to conflict with *your* show schedule," she said with a laugh. "I'd love to come watch. It's a plan!"

😂

Amy stood waving as Ben drove off, feeling much happier. It was good to have cleared the air with him. As his pickup disappeared in a cloud of dust, she started thinking about the day ahead. *Venture's first acupuncture session,* she thought, and felt a thrill of excitement. It was going to be fascinating, seeing a new way of treating the horses, but she also knew how much she had invested in the procedure on an emotional level. If it didn't work, she couldn't bear the thought of having let Sergeant García down.

She helped Joni finish with the mucking out and was just emptying the wheelbarrow when she heard the familiar sound of Scott's Jeep coming up the driveway. She remembered that he had decided to come and watch the first acupuncture session.

"Hi Amy," Scott called, slamming the Jeep door. "I know I'm a bit early, but I thought I'd drop in and see Lou. How's the patient?"

Amy shook her head. "Not much change," she said. "I'm not sure where we'll turn if the acupuncture doesn't make a difference." She gazed questioningly at Scott. "I know you don't think there's much chance . . ."

Scott looked serious. "Well, I didn't mean to sound so skeptical. I think it depends a lot on the particular horse and the particular problem," he said. "But like any other treatment, it's not guaranteed to work."

"Well, we don't even know if Dr. Janssen will think it's right for him," Amy added. "We just have to hope for the best."

Scott responded. "Everyone's pretty used to that around here."

Amy nodded, and spotted Joni watching them with an anxious expression. She went over. "When is your mom planning to be here?" Amy asked. "Your uncle's bringing her over from Baltimore, isn't he?"

"She should be here soon," Joni replied, taking a deep

breath. "Say, Amy, if acupuncture's not right for Venture, there's probably something else that'll work for him, you know."

"Don't worry. I'll understand if your mom doesn't want to do it," Amy reassured her. "Venture's had every treatment under the sun. It'll be amazing if this works for him. If it doesn't, we'll just have to find what does."

Joni looked relieved. "Well, we'll just have to see what Mom decides," she said. "Fingers crossed!"

They both turned at the sound of another car coming up the driveway. "That's my uncle's car," said Joni.

A silver Chrysler pulled into the front yard. Joni ran forward to the passenger side and Dr. Janssen climbed out. Amy watched as she gave Joni a big hug. She was struck by how much Greta looked like her daughter; but she was taller, and her straight blond hair was shorter, cropped in a short tousled style. The man who got out of the driver's seat could only be Greta's brother, a few years older perhaps, but with the same blond hair and smiling eyes.

"You must be Amy," said Dr. Janssen. "I've heard so much about you." She held out her hand. "Greta Janssen — and this is my brother, Leif."

Amy smiled and shook hands. Lou and Scott came out of the farmhouse and Ty appeared from the feed room, so Amy did a round of introductions. Once they were over, Leif climbed back into his car, saying he'd be back in a couple of hours, and drove off with a cheery wave.

"Would you like a coffee or anything before you meet Venture?" Amy asked Greta.

"Oh, I'm fine for now." Greta smiled. "I'm interested in seeing your patient more than anything. But a coffee when I've finished would be just great!"

"I'll leave you to it," said Ty. "We don't want to overwhelm Venture with visitors." He reached out to touch Amy's hand before heading off to the feed room. "Good luck," he added.

Amy led Scott, Joni, and Greta across the front yard. Greta stopped at each stable door to greet the horses. Joni had obviously told her all about them. Amy felt a pang as she realized how much Greta and her own mother would have had in common, and how much they would have liked each other.

They reached Venture's stall and Amy slid back the bolt. As usual, the police horse was standing at the back. He rolled the whites of his eyes nervously at the group of people entering his stall. Amy went to his head to try and reassure him.

"I think I'll watch from outside," said Joni. "It's a bit crowded and the needles aren't even out yet." Joni claimed a spot leaning over the half door instead.

As Greta began to study the horse, Amy quickly ran

through his history, explaining how it was impossible to tell the extent of his physical pain because he seemed so depressed.

Greta nodded. "So, nonspecific pain, probably in the back region, combined with the effects of trauma." She turned to Scott. "Is there anything else you can tell me?"

Scott shook his head. "No. He's had thorough spinal checks and extensive medical treatment for weeks. There doesn't seem to be anything else physical that I can help you with."

Greta stepped forward and placed her hand lightly on the police horse's back. He shifted uneasily, his ears flattened. Greta began to press with one finger more firmly in particular places, watching Venture's reaction. Sometimes he exhibited more uneasiness, at other times less.

"At the moment, I'm just looking for problem spots, assessing which meridians need unblocking," she explained to Scott and Amy. "I would say from his reactions so far that acupuncture could definitely offer him a way forward. There's one particular set of points that seems to be provoking a response in him. Is it OK with you if I go ahead?"

"Yes, please," said Amy. "It won't hurt him, will it?"

Greta smiled. "No. The most he'll feel is a dull tingling when I put the needles in. At least that's all humans ever say they feel. Once they're in, you might be surprised at how much he relaxes."

"How long do you keep them in?" asked Scott as Greta opened her case and selected one of the fine, sterile needles.

"It varies from horse to horse," said Greta. "In Venture's case, I'll probably leave them there for twenty minutes or so. Perhaps a little longer."

Expertly, she began to insert a series of needles into different points on Venture's neck and back. Amy counted nine altogether. She watched, fascinated, as Greta stepped back for a moment, then gently manipulated the needles one at a time. Amy threw a quick glance at Joni, who was leaning over the half door looking a lot less anxious than Amy felt.

After a few moments, Amy realized that Venture's eyes had begun to close.

"He's falling asleep," she whispered.

Greta nodded. "That often happens. He'll probably remain drowsy for a while afterward, too."

Amy stroked Venture's nose in wonderment. She hadn't seen him looking this relaxed in his entire stay at Heartland. She grinned at Joni, and the stable girl grinned back, her blue eyes sparkling.

After about twenty-five minutes, Greta quietly removed the needles and packed them away. She stroked Venture's neck for a moment. "Well, that's it," she said. "All done for now. I'm going to be around for a few days, so I can come back on Monday and Wednesday, if that's convenient for you. Three treatments should help him a lot. After that, Joni can continue with acupressure on the same points — as long as she follows my instructions closely, it will be almost as beneficial as the needles."

Joni's face lit up. "Is that OK, Amy?" she asked. "I've got my preliminary qualification. I'll make sure that Mom talks me through the meridians she's stimulating."

"So, acupressure just uses finger pressure in the same places where she put the needles, right?" Amy checked. She glanced at Scott. "That should be fine, shouldn't it?"

Scott nodded. "Yeah, it sounds good to me," he said. "I have to say, I'm very impressed with Venture's reaction. It makes me wonder about the training myself."

They all stepped out of the stall, leaving Venture with his eyes half shut and his lower lip drooping, a sure sign that he had drifted off happily. Amy stayed to take one last look at him as the others made their way to the farmhouse to tell Lou and Jack the good news.

"You're going to get better, Venture," she whispered. "It's been a long journey, but we'll get there soon."

Chapter Twelve

Lou placed a fresh plateful of muffins on the table, then sat down again. "I've asked Nancy to come to Ben's good-bye party next Saturday," she said casually. "And she said yes."

Jack and Amy stopped eating and looked at her in surprise. Jack's face broke into a grin. "That was nice of you, Lou," he said. "I'm sure she'd love to come."

Amy caught her sister's eye and gave her a soft smile of reassurance.

"She said she wasn't sure, at first." Lou looked self-consciously at her slice of toast. "But I told her she should consider herself part of the family now."

Amy looked at their grandfather to see how he would react. He didn't say anything, but he reached out and squeezed Lou's hand. Amy felt glad and also realized that Lou's words were true: Nancy *was* part of the family. She wasn't taking anyone's place, but her presence brought a new warmth and energy to the house. And she was clearly very important to Grandpa. Amy quickly threw a smile at Ty, who was sitting quietly next to her. He was offering the silent support she had grown to rely on. She wanted to tell him that he was part of the family, too, but she didn't quite know how. Amy touched his hand and gave it a squeeze.

He turned and looked at her. Seeing his gaze, Amy knew he understood.

It was Sunday morning. Joni had taken the day off to visit with her mother, so it was just the four of them sitting at the brunch table. When they had finished eating, Ty and Amy did the dishes together, then headed out onto the yard.

"Venture's definitely looking brighter today," commented Ty as they approached his stall. "But I guess there's still a long way to go before we could even think about saddling him again."

Venture looked around with his ears pricked as they peered into his stall. It was true: the lines of his body did seem more relaxed, and his expression was curious for a change.

"I'll take him for a gentle walk down to the paddock today," said Ty. "It's a nice day. He could stay out for a bit. What time is Eloise coming for Molly?"

"Anytime now," said Amy. "I'll miss her. She's a star."

She fetched a broom and began to sweep the front yard. Within a few minutes, Molly had left her hay net and was watching Amy over her half door, her intelligent eyes following Amy's every movement.

"Hey there, Molly," laughed Amy, stopping to scratch her neck. "It's almost home time for you. Did you know that?"

As Molly snorted and blew over her hair, Amy heard the sound of a Jeep and trailer rattling up the drive. "In fact," she said to the horse, "it might be sooner rather than later. I think that's your owner now."

Sure enough, it was Eloise who jumped out of the driver's seat, grinning. She walked over to Amy and reached up to give Molly a stroke on the nose.

"Hi, Eloise," said Amy. "She's all yours again. I'll go and grab her tack."

"Thanks, Amy," responded Eloise. "I'm so excited to be taking her home. I can't wait to get her out on the trails again."

Amy jogged over to the tack room and picked out Molly's tack and blankets. With the bridle slung over her shoulder and the saddle hoisted onto her arm, she marched back out again. Then she stopped. Eloise had led Molly out of her stall and was giving the mare a big hug around the neck.

Amy smiled. She had built a strong bond of trust

working with the mare — but there was no doubt who Molly loved most of all.

❧

Amy watched as Greta Janssen laid out her case of needles inside Venture's stall. It was Wednesday, and Greta had arrived to do the third acupuncture session. "I think Sergeant García will be showing up soon," Amy said. "He was interested to see one of the sessions. I suggested he come to this one, if that's OK with you?"

"Fine," said Greta. "I hope he's not expecting miracles, though. It's going to take this fellow a long time to get back to full form. The sergeant needs to realize that."

Amy smiled. "I think any change at all will seem like a miracle to Sergeant García," she said. "He's been really patient. He just needs a little good news."

Venture was looking a lot more lively and more attentive to what was going on around him. In the last five days, the sense of stiffness and pain in his body had begun to ease quite visibly. When Greta had arrived, he had actually whickered a gentle welcome, as though he knew she would bring him comfort.

"I've shown Joni exactly what I'm doing so that she'll be able to continue with acupressure after I've gone," said Greta, as she began the careful process of inserting the needles. Joni watched closely. "Acupressure is very effective and relaxing."

"I tried T-touch, but he hated it," said Amy, puzzled. "You do that with pressure from your fingers, too. Why should acupressure be different?"

"T-touch isn't based on the meridians and points," Greta explained. "It's relaxing, but it's not working with the body's channels of energy in the same way. Acupressure doesn't work along the surface of the skin — it's triggering the points underneath it."

Amy looked up as a shadow fell across the door. It was Sergeant García. He looked astonished to see the arrangement of needles sticking out of Venture but stood quietly outside, his eyes wide, as Greta manipulated each one in turn. By the time she took them out again, Venture had started to doze off.

As Greta packed away her needles, Amy invited the sergeant to come inside the stall.

"Greta, this is Sergeant García, Venture's rider," she said.

Greta shook his hand and smiled. "Venture's a fine horse," she told him warmly. "I think he may be on the mend now."

The sergeant stroked Venture's neck. "I can already see a change," he said. "Thank you. I can't tell you how much this means to me. It would be amazing to see him healthy again."

His face broke into a smile, and Amy handed him Venture's lead rope. "He's quite sleepy at the moment," she said. "But maybe you'd like to walk down to the paddock with him later?"

"I might do that," said Mark. "Thanks." Amy nodded to him and returned the smile.

Amy then took Joni and Greta to the farmhouse, where Lou had some coffee brewing. Joni was looking a little sad, as this was her mother's last evening before going back to Canada.

"Would you like to stay for supper?" Lou offered. "There's plenty of food."

"That's very kind, but no, thank you," said Greta. "I have an early morning flight, so I need to get back to my brother's."

"Well, it's been great meeting you," said Lou. "I'm sure we'll see you again, now that Joni's working here."

"Of course. And I'll be expecting Joni to give me detailed updates on Venture's progress," Greta replied, putting down her coffee cup. "I must be going." She shrugged on her coat. "Good-bye. And see you soon."

Amy accompanied Greta and Joni outside, then left them to say good-bye to each other. She wondered how Sergeant García and Venture were doing, so she wandered over to his stall. Finding it empty, she walked down the track toward the paddock.

In the early evening light, the sergeant was leading the horse along one side of the top paddock, one hand on the dark brown neck for reassurance. Venture was striding out calmly, his neck arched and his ears pricked forward.

Amy held back, not wanting to disturb them. Their silhouette was so peaceful in the twilight. She watched for a moment longer, then slipped away, her heart full of hope. Through all the changes that had taken place — Ben leaving, Joni arriving — they had found a solution for Venture's problem. The police horse still had a long road before him, but at least he had made the first step. Next Amy thought of Sergeant García and his ability to believe that Venture would recover. The sergeant had placed faith in Heartland and had even invested his own money. Amy was inspired by his dedication and had every hope that he and Venture would be working together again soon.

🙠

"Ben won the blue ribbon!" Amy called out cheerily, opening the kitchen door. She was greeted by a blast of heat, a noticeable contrast to the cold air outside. It was Saturday. Lou and Nancy were bustling around with their cheeks flushed, the preparations for the evening's dinner well under way. Nancy was rinsing a big pile of blueberries, while Lou was stirring something on the stove.

"Hey, that's great!" exclaimed Lou. "So it's a double celebration!"

"He's on cloud nine," laughed Amy, going over to peer into Lou's saucepan. It was full of a rich chili sauce that smelled wonderful. "What can I do to help?"

Nancy and Lou both called out orders at the same time.

"You can grate some cheese for the tortillas," said Lou.

"You can roll out the crust for my pie," Nancy suggested.

Amy looked from one to the other and laughed. "Are you going to fight over me?"

Lou grinned. "I think you should do Nancy's pastry," she said. "The cheese can wait until the last minute."

Feeling unexpectedly happy, Amy started in with the rolling pin. Things were certainly different when Nancy was around, and it was a relief that she and Lou were getting along again. Lost in her reflections, Amy failed to notice that her strip of pastry was turning out far too long and thin, and would never cover a pie tin.

"Hmmm," said Nancy good-humoredly when she saw Amy's handiwork. "I can see that cooking isn't your strong point. Maybe we should banish you to the stables. What d'you think, Lou?"

Lou laughed. "Nothing would make Amy happier," she teased.

❧

There was barely enough room for everyone when they sat down to eat — and certainly not enough room for all the food. Lou had made a Mexican feast of nachos and soft tortillas to fill with the delicious chili sauce, and lots of toppings.

"My favorite," declared Ben, sitting down next to Joni.

"How could I forget?" Lou answered with a laugh. Ben had never been shy about food.

Amy squeezed herself onto the kitchen bench between Ty and Grandpa and looked around happily. Joni was chatting with Ben about the show that day while Scott, who had just arrived, was washing his hands at the sink. Lou was hurriedly putting serving spoons in all the bowls.

Ty began filling up Amy's plate for her. "Guacamole?" he asked, holding a giant green spoonful over her plate.

Amy nodded. "Please. And lots of sour cream and cheese."

It was all delicious. Amy took a handful of crunchy nachos and passed the bowl to Grandpa and Nancy, who was just sitting down next to him.

"Now don't let me forget that pie," said Nancy. "It needs to stay in the oven for another fifteen minutes.

Any more and Amy's pastry will be burned." She smiled at Amy and gave her a wink.

Amy laughed. "It's good to have you back, Nancy," she said.

"Why, thank you, Amy," replied Nancy. "It's good to be back. And it's great to know we can get everything out in the open. I think you and Lou have a lot of courage. You must be proud of them, Jack."

Jack nodded. "Sure am," he said, giving Amy a grin.

Amy paused between bites to take it all in. Nancy's gracious words had warmed her to the core. She was so glad that Grandpa had found someone special after all this time . . . and however hard it might be, it was good to realize how much they had in common, too.

The feast was soon devoured, and Nancy began to get the next stage under way. Just as she placed her magnificent blueberry pie on the table, Lou cleared her throat to catch everyone's attention. Amy saw her exchange a meaningful glance with Scott. She wondered what was going on.

"Before we have dessert, Scott and I would like to say something," said Lou.

Everyone went quiet and listened expectantly.

"First of all, congratulations to Ben for winning today," Lou carried on. "And good luck for the future. I hope you'll come back . . ." She stopped speaking as everyone applauded.

Ben grinned happily and raised his glass. "Thank you, everybody."

". . . and I especially hope you'll come back on our wedding day," finished Lou, a bold blush coloring her face. "Scott and I have made a decision. We're going to get married in the fall."

There was a thunder of noise as everyone banged their spoons against their glasses and cheered.

Then Scott got to his feet, looking nervous. "There's just one more thing," he said. He turned to face Jack. "We'd like to use this happy occasion to ask your permission to be married at Heartland. It means so much to us, in so many ways, we can't imagine a better place to start the rest of our lives together."

Jack looked stunned, then a huge smile spread across his face. He got up and gave Lou and Scott each a hug. Amy sneaked a look at Nancy and caught her wiping away a tear.

"Nothing would give me more pleasure," said Grandpa. With a quick glance at Nancy, he added, "I'm so proud of both Lou and Amy. I'm lucky to have two wonderful granddaughters. And to see one of you getting happily married is the most wonderful thing I could ever hope for." He cleared his throat and reached for his glass. "To Lou and Scott."

"To Lou and Scott!" everyone chorused.

"And to happy futures," added Jack. "For those leaving and those arriving. We wish you all the very best. To happy futures!"

"To happy futures!" rang out around the table.

❧

Later, as they waved Ben and Joni good-bye in the yard, Amy went over to Ty and leaned against him. He smiled and put his arm around her.

"So much change," Amy murmured. "But I'm glad we're both still here."

"I don't have plans to go anywhere else," said Ty.

Amy sighed. "You were right about Ben," she said. "Heartland isn't right for everyone, not forever. People have to move on — just like horses. And neither is easy."

Ty pulled her closer to him. "But it can be good," he pointed out. "It can be really good."

Amy thought of Joni and smiled, and she looked across the yard and saw Nancy chatting happily with Lou and Scott. She had no doubt Nancy had some new ideas about the wedding to share. The Heartland family kept shifting and moving on . . . but however much it changed, there was always something worth holding on to, something they could all believe in — something they could all hold dear.